Marc d'Angelo wasn't at all what she'd expected....

Behind that sweaty, muscular chest was a man who actually *cared* about her and Tyler. Maybe she'd misjudged him.

And the more she thought about it, the more Paige realized that not only was her four-year-old son in awe of this stranger, but she was falling for him, too—and fast.

Suddenly the building and the noise weren't all that bad when she considered the alternative… never having met her sexy new neighbor at all. And as far as forever went, well, she'd just have to see about that, because Marc wasn't going *anywhere*, and Tyler was already thinking "daddy."

Thanks to Marc, the walls were certainly crumbling down around her hardened heart….

Dear Reader,

This book was inspired by reality. My husband and I had just bought a one-hundred-year-old duplex in the area of Toronto called "Cabbagetown"—so named for the boiled cabbage that was a diet staple of the Irish laborers who lived in that part of town at the turn of the century. It had been renovated, as had many of the homes in the area, and one inside wall had been taken right back to the bare brick. It looked gorgeous, but it kept "molting" pieces of mortar and bits of rotted brick, and I spent the whole time we lived there expecting to walk into the living room one day and find a hole through into the attached home on the other side of the wall. It never happened, but it started me thinking...gee, what if...? And this book was born. Paige came to me first, and I realized that it was going to take a very special man to win her heart. I've always loved big families, so I knew Marc had a mob of brothers and sisters. And it was important to have someone so comfortable with family and the concept of sharing and caring for those around you that he'd just walk into her life and take over because it was completely natural for him to do so. Like her father, he's motivated by all the right reasons—it's just that his enthusiasm gets away from him now and again. I loved writing this book— all the characters were great fun, and I was sorry to have to leave them when I got to the end. I just hope you enjoy it as much as I did!

Sincerely,

Naomi Horton

NAOMI HORTON
No Walls Between Us

Silhouette Books

Published by Silhouette Books

America's Publisher of Contemporary Romance

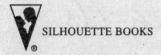

SILHOUETTE BOOKS

ISBN-13: 978-0-373-36131-1
ISBN-10:   0-373-36131-9

NO WALLS BETWEEN US

NAOMI HORTON

Naomi Horton was born in northern Alberta, where the winters are long and the libraries far apart. "When I'd run out of books," she says, "I'd simply create my own—entire worlds filled with people, adventure and romance. I guess it's not surprising that I'm still at it!" This RITA® Award-winning author is an engineering technologist who presently lives in Nanaimo, British Columbia, with her collection of assorted pets.

For Sharon Singer, who gave me the idea;
Marilyn Field (the best real estate agent in
the world), who gave me the inspiration; the old
house on Geneva Avenue, which gave me the
firsthand experience.

One

It was a scream that woke Paige. Thin, shrill, as though torn from the throat of a soul in torment, it jolted her out of the first decent sleep she'd had all week. She sat up with a gasp, the hair on the back of her neck starting to lift until she realized what it was. Power saw.

She dropped back down against the pillow with a groan and squeezed her eyes shut, willing sleep to return. The scream of the saw reached a crescendo, so loud she half expected to see the whirling blade slice through her bedroom wall. It didn't, of course. But when the banshee wail stopped after a moment, Paige found herself relaxing. She opened one eye and looked at the digital clock glowing on her bedside table. Minutes after six. In the morning.

He's crazy, she found herself thinking idly as she

watched spangles of morning sunlight play across the ceiling. I'm sharing the house with a crazy man.

Sharing, thank heaven, wasn't quite the right word. The huge old house had been divided into two separate residences years ago, so in reality she and her neighbor shared nothing but a common wall. But it was just on the other side of that wall that her new neighbor was doing whatever he was doing. Ripping the place apart brick by brick, by the sound of it, Paige decided, irritated. She glanced at the clock again and sighed. As she did every morning, she toyed with the idea of staying in bed. It would be so nice just to curl up and pull the covers over her head, to slide back into the safety and undemanding comfort of sleep.

Eyes closed, Paige smiled grimly. It was too late for that. Almost three years ago, in the weeks right after her husband, Peter, had been killed, she'd done just that, using sleep to avoid facing the truth, preferring the nightmares of her mind to the nightmares of reality. But she'd discovered the hard way that sleep only postpones; it doesn't cure.

Footsteps. Adrift in that dreamlike haze between sleep and wakefulness, Paige listened to those loud, determined footsteps for a long while before it dawned on her that they were real—and before she realized where they were coming from. Her eyes snapped open, and she stared disbelievingly at the ceiling. Someone was in the attic. *Her* attic.

She sat bolt upright, eyes following the invisible invader as he made his way across the room upstairs. He reached the far wall, then turned and came back again, pausing now and again as though examining something. The floor joists creaked alarmingly as the intruder stepped carefully from one to the other, and Paige found herself holding her breath. One misstep and he'd come crashing through the thin plaster ceiling, right on top of her. The footsteps passed over her head again and disappeared into her neighbor's side of the attic, and Paige eased her breath out.

"What does he think he's doing!" She flung herself out of bed, naked and furious, muttering an oath as she snatched up a handful of clothing and stormed down to the bathroom.

The domed skylight set in the ceiling right above the stairwell was ablaze with early-morning light, and, as she did every time she walked under it, Paige felt some of her tension evaporate. She loved that skylight. It was one of the reasons she'd bought this house. Even on the most overcast day, it flooded the stairwell and narrow upstairs corridor with warmth and light, giving them and the living room below a feeling of airiness.

She lifted her face to the sun's gentle warmth, smiling. And found herself looking at a complete stranger.

She couldn't see him clearly against the brightness, but she knew it was a man. He seemed to be kneeling beside the skylight, and as she stared up at him in disbelief, he got to his feet. He stood there for a moment, etched clearly against the brilliant blue sky, then turned and vanished into the sun. Paige blinked, then listened in growing anger as receding footsteps crunched across the roof. *Her* roof, she reminded herself furiously. Damn it, it was her roof! It was only then that she remembered she was stark naked.

She gave the skylight one horrified look, then scampered into the safety of the bathroom, cheeks burning. Enough is enough, she told herself furiously. Waking her up at six in the morning was bad enough. Wandering through her attic and across her roof as though he owned the place was even worse. But if he thought for a minute that he was going to get away with spying on her through her own skylight, he was in for the surprise of his life.

She'd never met her neighbor, aside from catching a glimpse now and again of someone tall and dark-haired. She knew he'd bought his side of the house months ago but hadn't lived in it until now and that he drove a bright red Porsche and a battered old pickup truck with equal panache. He'd seemed nice enough. In fact, she'd decided it was time to go over and introduce herself and maybe even invite him over for a neighborly drink. Until this morning, that is. Now she still intended to go over and introduce herself, but it would be to lay down the law about his fetish for predawn carpentry and skylights. To hell with being a good neighbor!

The faucet squealed in protest when she turned the shower on, and the pipes rattled ominously all the way to the basement, where the hot-water tank sat gurgling. But nothing exploded or expired noisily on the spot, and she breathed a little easier as she gathered her thick chestnut hair into a knot and pinned it securely. No two ways about it, one of these days she was going to have to get the ancient plumbing overhauled. She winced just thinking about it. The last estimate on replacing the entire system had left her pale with shock and resigned to showering in rusty, lukewarm water. She loved her half of this old house, but obviously it was going to try her patience to the utmost.

As was the idiot next door.

She showered swiftly, having learned from unhappy experience that dawdling meant spending the last few minutes in cold water. But this morning she was lucky, and by the time she was finished, the water was only uncomfortably cool. She toweled herself dry briskly, pulled on blue jeans and a pale blue chambray shirt, and put her thick, shoulder-length hair up into a loose ponytail.

There was an extra-loud crash from the other side of the wall. Paige winced, holding her breath. But there was no agonized cry of pain, and after a moment she released her breath with a mutter of profanity and finished stuffing the shirttails into her jeans. She threaded her narrow leather belt through the loops and buckled it as she headed down the corridor toward her son's bedroom, remembering just in time not to slam the bathroom door behind her. She'd have loved to slam it hard enough to crack plaster, but the momentary satisfaction it would give her would be offset by the fact it would also waken Tyler. And this morning she could use some extra time to herself before she got him up. She had a thousand things to do and not nearly enough time, as usual.

Even thinking about the day ahead made her stomach tighten. She'd been worked to the bone for the past two months trying to get GingerBread Preserves off the ground, but it had been even worse since the sales of her homemade jams, preserves and condiments had started to take off. Paige smiled wryly, thinking of the old Chinese saying: "Be careful what you wish for, because it might come true." Wishing alone hadn't turned GingerBread Preserves into a moderate success, of course. It had been perseverance, stubbornness and countless fourteen-hour days. But it looked as though all that hard work was starting to pay off, and GingerBread Preserves, if not exactly thriving, was at least holding its head above water.

Paige opened the door to her son's bedroom. Tyler was still sound asleep, covers kicked off, small face flushed with sleep, mouth uplifted with the angelic smile that fooled everyone but Paige. In another hour or two he'd be up roaring through her life like a tornado, filled with an energy and enthusiasm that amazed her. She smiled, wishing there were some way to cork some of that energy into small glass bottles and sell it alongside her preserves and jams.

Her smile faded. Poor Tyler. These past few months had been harder on him than they'd been on her. At least she understood why she was working those fourteen-hour days without a break, why she had so little time to spend with him. She knew that once GingerBread Preserves was a going concern and she could afford to hire some help, she'd have plenty of time to play with him again. But Tyler didn't understand that. All he knew was that his mother was hardly around and that when she was around, she was often preoccupied and short-tempered, and she never seemed to want to play anymore.

"I'm sorry, Tyler," she whispered. "It'll be better in another six months." Either way, she added to herself. Because in six months either she'd be successful enough to have help, or she'd be bankrupt.

She tucked the sheet around Tyler, pausing long enough to kiss his moist, warm cheek. Then she withdrew and closed his door.

Another crash reverberated through the house, making her jump. She held her breath again, listening not for a cry of pain but a howl of outrage from Tyler. When no sound came from his bedroom, she relaxed, shaking her head wonderingly at his ability to sleep through what sounded like Armageddon. What *was* that maniac next door doing at this hour, anyway?

She was going to kill him, she decided quite calmly as she walked toward the stairs. Justifiable homicide, they'd call it. Any man who started rebuilding his house at six in the morning deserved to be throttled with the cord of his own power saw.

She was halfway downstairs when she heard the first bricks fall. They hit hardwood flooring with three distinct thuds, followed by what sounded like cascading pebbles and a snarl of profanity. At first she thought it had come from the other side of the wall, and she smiled a trifle maliciously. She didn't wish him any ill will, exactly, but a broken toe or two might put a damper on his early-morning activities.

Then she saw the bricks. Three of them. They lay on the hardwood floor of her living room, surrounded by a sprinkling of plaster. But it wasn't the bricks that held Paige's attention; it was the hole in her newly painted living-room wall—a three-brick-size hole at about shoulder height that was still dribbling red dust and chunks of mortar.

Paige stared at it disbelievingly. This couldn't be happening. She and Tyler had spent most of the week at her parents' because of that wall. Or rather, because of the mess raised by the crew of workmen she'd brought in to repair the damage done to it by the previous owner's Great Dane. Her eyes widened even more when, without warning, a plaster-coated hand poked through the hole. It groped through air right in front of her, turning this way and that as though trying to find something solid to latch on to. There was another mutter of profanity, more heartfelt than before, and without even thinking about what she was doing, Paige reached out and grabbed the hand by the wrist.

"You idiot!" she nearly shouted, giving the hand a ferocious yank. "You just broke my wall!"

She heard a startled inhalation from the other side of the wall. So fast she didn't even have time to react, the hand twisted around and grabbed her wrist in a steel grip. Paige gave a yelp and stared at the strong fingers welded around her wrist. "What do you think you're doing?" she asked in a squeaky whisper.

There was no answer. Feeling like a character in Alice's Wonderland, Paige hesitantly peeked through the hole. She half expected to come face to face with a worried white rabbit, but there was nothing on the other side except a naked, sweat-streaked male chest. She blinked stupidly at it. Then, in the next instant, she was staring into two of the bluest eyes she'd ever seen in her life. Which decidedly was not what she would have expected to find staring back at her through a hole in her living-room wall.

The eyes locked with hers, wide with astonishment. Then, suddenly, they filled with gentle amusement and Paige heard a rumbling chuckle. "Well, well," purred a delicious male baritone from just beyond the hole. "What *have* we got here?"

Paige gaped at him. As she slowly gathered her wits, she sucked in an outraged breath. "You idiot! Look what you've done to my wall! And let go of me!" She emphasized the last word with a tremendous wrench of her arm.

Caught off balance, the stranger gave a yell of surprise and fell against the wall so solidly that the entire house shuddered. A huge section of plaster bulged outward and began to crack and shatter, and Paige stared disbelievingly as half the wall seemed to melt. A cascade of plaster, crumbling bricks and mortar poured across her floor, raising a thick cloud of dust. And in the middle of it, coated with plaster and red brick dust, rose the ghostlike figure of a man.

He gazed at the ruin around him as though not quite sure what had happened, then looked around at her. He was smeared with plaster dust and cobwebs and was bleeding slightly from a long shallow cut on his right cheek. He touched it gingerly, looking at his bloodied fingers in surprise, and then, to Paige's utter astonishment, that handsome dusty face broke into a huge, impudent grin. "Hi."

"You—you broke my wall," she whispered in a small, accusing voice.

The tall stranger looked around. "I'd planned on inviting myself over for a drink sometime this week anyway."

"Drink?" Paige echoed. He looked like a tall savage standing there, his naked shoulders and chest streaked with ocher war paint where the brick and plaster dust had combined with his sweat.

"Yeah." The grin turned raffish, and he wiped his hand on his denim-clad thigh and extended it toward her. "I'm Marc d'Angelo. You must be Paige MacKenzie."

Paige stared at the outstretched hand. "I want you and your mess out of my house, Mr. d'Angelo," she said with astonishing calm. "I have a business appointment at ten, and by the time I get back I expect to find my wall repaired, plastered and painted."

"Can't paint wet plaster," he advised. "And it's going to take more than an afternoon to repair this." He stepped cautiously through the rubble and tugged at a protruding brick. It came free and he held it toward her. "Porous as sponge candy; disintegrates if you even look at it." When it was obvious that Paige wasn't going to take it, he tossed the brick onto the pile at his feet, then wiped both hands on his thighs and stared up and around at the jagged edges of the hole. "Looks like this used to be an arched doorway once." He poked at a loose brick, grunting when it and the mortar around it crumbled. "Lousy workmanship. Whoever did the work either didn't care or was just plain stupid." He pulled another brick free and tossed it down with the rest. "All this will have to be cleaned out." His gesture took in the entire ragged hole. "Taken right back to solid brick, if there is any. If we try to fill this in without anchoring the new brickwork to something solid, it'll just cave in again. Maybe seriously hurt someone next time."

"Someone's going to be seriously hurt if this mess isn't cleaned up by the time I get home," Paige said angrily. "It's bad enough that you start whatever you're doing in there before the sun's even up, but now you've destroyed my entire living room."

"You were the one who pulled me through the wall," her war-painted companion reminded her. "And it was after six when I started work this morning."

"Five minutes after six," Paige added, feeling her temper rising in spite of her best efforts to control it. "Didn't it occur to you that you just *might* be disturbing whoever lives on this side?"

The laughter had gone from d'Angelo's mouth by now, and he looked at her with faint impatience. "It occurred to me. That's why I've been getting up at five and working past midnight every day this week, trying to get the heavy stuff done while you and your son were at your parents'." Blue eyes met hers through the faint haze of dust still hanging in the air. "You weren't supposed to be back until tomorrow."

He made it sound as though it was her fault, Paige thought furiously. And just how did he know so much about her? "Are you going to clean this up?"

"In time." A hint of laughter brushed his mouth again. It was a good mouth, Paige had to admit. A strong mouth, made for laughter and for drinking wine and for kissing... She gave herself a mental shake. "I would suggest," she told him in the tone of voice her mother used on recalcitrant repairmen and snippy salesclerks, "that you find time to do it immediately."

The Voice, as her father called it, didn't have the desired effect on Marc d'Angelo. Immune to its implied threat, he simply stared down at her as though amused by her outrage. "Four o'clock," she said through gritted teeth. "I'll give you until four o'clock to have the hole repaired and this mess cleaned up." Her back ramrod stiff, she turned on her heel and stalked across the living room and into the small galley kitchen.

As he watched her walk away, Marc was torn between frank admiration and an overwhelming urge to laugh. By God, she was something else! She was the spitting image of Bub about twelve years ago, he thought with an amused shake of his head. When his sister had brought home the tiny ginger kitten, Beelzebub, late one evening, the entire family had gathered around to stare down at it. Bub had puffed himself up into a passing imitation of a real cat and had spat and growled at anything that moved, making such a fierce show in spite of his size that he'd earned his name and everyone's loving respect on the spot.

Marc's smile turned rueful, and he absently rubbed the scars on the back of his hand. Bub's ferocity hadn't been all playacting. And there had been something in the glint in Paige MacKenzie's eyes a few minutes ago that made him think hers wasn't, either.

It was then that he realized he was still standing up to his ankles in plaster dust and bricks, grinning idiotically at absolutely nothing. He wiped the silly smile off his mouth and gave his head another shake, one of mild annoyance at himself this time. He looked around him with growing despair. You really did it this time, hotshot. Pop was right. You *have* been away from the nuts-and-bolts end of the construction business for too long. You'd never have messed up like this while you were still working for him, that's for sure.

Marc winced, thinking about what Vincenzo d'Angelo was going to have to say about this when he saw it. Not entirely without reason, he reminded himself with another wince. Sixteen years of office work, sixteen years of never getting closer to a construction site than a set of blueprints and a contractor's report, had made him sloppy. Pop had noticed the change in him right away and hadn't wasted a minute telling him about it. "You lost the touch," he'd said in disgust just last night. "I trained you good, Marco. Like Roman, like Gabriel. I trained all my boys good, but you—you I trained the best. Roman and Gabriel are good builders, but they don't have what you had. You always had the eye for it, Marco, the touch. But now…" His father had made a gesture of dismissal. "You've spent too much time working with a pencil instead of a hammer."

He could be right, Marc found himself brooding for about the hundredth time in the past month. He looked down at his flat, tanned belly with satisfaction and flexed his shoulders, relishing the ripple of newly toned muscle. Four weeks ago he'd been in sorry shape, fifteen pounds overweight and flabby. He'd taken up swimming again, and jogging, but it had been the long days of back-breaking work with his father's construction company that had done him the most good. He was getting back in touch with himself, back in touch with what was important in life. But one thing was certain: It wasn't going to be half as easy as he'd thought it would be.

He brushed plaster dust off his jeans. He didn't quite know what he was trying to prove. Or even who he was trying to prove it to. All he did know was that during the next couple of months he had to make a decision about where his life was going. He was a good structural engineer, but he honestly didn't know if he wanted to go back to the world of blueprints and contractual negotiations again. It had killed his partner, and it had been the realization that it could kill him, too, that had gotten him out of that rat race.

Marc sighed and gazed around him. Pop wanted him to take over the family construction business. The thought of it gave him a feeling of excitement he hadn't had in years, but he couldn't help but ask himself if it would last. Would he really be happy with dirt under his nails, or would the magic fade, leaving him jaded and bored and at loose ends again?

Hell, he thought, disgruntled. I'm too old for all this adolescent angst! And too young to be going through midlife crisis.

In spite of himself, he smiled. Maybe Angelica was right. Maybe he *was* getting old. And maybe buying this sorry excuse for a house was part of what his sister had called his ''maturing process.'' She'd said it was a sign he was ready to start the next stage of his life, that he'd simply answered some ancient biological urge to find a cave and settle down. A woman will be next, she'd teased him. *The* woman. Then kids. Then a station wagon in the driveway instead of the candy-apple-red Porsche that sat there now. In a word, domesticity. Oddly enough, instead of dismissing her musings with a laugh, he'd found the idea more intriguing than he'd have thought befitting a wily old bachelor like him.

Marc chuckled, staring at the bricks surrounding him. So far he wasn't doing too well. Two weeks in the place and he'd brought the cave down around his ears and had antagonized his biological opposite in the other half to the point where she was undoubtedly contemplating murder. Much more ''domesticity'' and he could give up on the station wagon idea. His Porsche would be more than adequate transportation for a good many years to come.

He found himself grinning again and glanced toward the kitchen. He couldn't see Paige, but he could hear her muttering to herself, banging pots and pans around, slamming cupboard doors. She might not be very big, but she could sure pack a lot of mad into what was there. A whole lot of woman, too, he mused, thinking of the surprisingly lush curves her faded jeans had encased, the promising thrust of her small, high breasts against the soft cotton shirt. He found himself remembering how he'd glanced idly through the skylight this morning and seen her below him, naked and golden. She'd vanished the instant he'd realized what he was looking at, but the image of her was still burned into his retinas as permanently as designs etched on glass. He felt a familiar, warm stirring inside and took a deep breath, shaking himself free of the seductive image. "Get to work," he growled under his breath. Much more of this and you'll wind up spending the rest of the morning under a cold shower.

He stooped down to go through the hole in the wall into his own side of the house when a movement at the top of the stairs caught his eye. He straightened slowly, smiling. "Hi."

A small boy stood on the top step, clutching a ragged yellow blanket in one hand and the railing in the other. His wheat-colored hair was still tousled from sleep. It glowed in the sun streaming down from the skylight, and he looked like a cherub in a Botticelli painting.

"What's your name?"

The boy thought that over for a moment, then moved down one step. "Tyler."

"Did we wake you up?"

"There was a big noise." He moved down another step, then a third. "What's your name?"

"Marc. Marc d'Angelo."

"An...gelo?" The small heart-shaped face broke into a cherubic smile. "Like a angel?"

Marc smiled. "You'd be one of the first to think so, but yeah, sort of like an angel."

Tyler padded down the rest of the steps trustingly. His pajama top was inside-out, and he seemed to be having trouble holding the bottoms up. At every step he had to let go of the railing and give them a tug. His eyes got wider and wider as he took in the hole in the wall and the surrounding mess. "It looks like a elephant broke it down." Those round eyes, the exact russet shade of his mother's, locked onto Marc's. "Did you do that?"

Marc winced. "Afraid so. Kind of a mess, isn't it?"

"Boy," Tyler said philosophically, "is my mom gonna be mad at you."

Marc chuckled, recalling Paige's ire. "Does your mom stay mad for long?"

"No." Tyler gave his pajama pants another hitch. "She hollers a lot, then kisses you and says it's all right. And maybe gives you a cookie."

"That sound promising."

"Don't count on it, Mr. d'Angelo." Paige's voice was cool, but when Marc glanced around, he could've sworn there was the slightest twinkle of amusement in her eyes as she walked toward them.

"What, no cookie?" Marc couldn't have broken her stare even if he'd wanted to, suddenly having the most breathtakingly vivid image of what it would be like to kiss this woman. She'd be as sweet as nectar, he knew, her mouth warm and liquid and alive under his, coaxing him in, teasing.

"Not even a crumb."

Yes, Marc thought, it was definitely a twinkle. He wondered if she had the slightest idea of the decidedly lustful thoughts that had been tumbling through his head since he'd first set eyes on her that morning. Thoughts that, frankly, surprised him as much as they'd have surprised her had she suspected them. He couldn't remember the last time a woman had affected him like this. He didn't exactly lead the life of a playboy—Angelica's caustic comments notwithstanding—but neither had he suffered from a lack of female companionship over the years. But it had been a long while since he'd met a woman who made him feel so alive, so…male. And it was, he decided, a nice feeling indeed.

He realized he was still staring at her. Her cheeks had taken on a faint pink tinge, as though she knew exactly what he'd been thinking, and he turned away abruptly. "I'll see you later," he growled, deciding he'd better get out of there before he was arrested on the strength of his mental imagery alone.

"Four o'clock, Mr. d'Angelo," she called after him. "If you don't have my wall fixed by then, you're in big trouble!"

But for some reason, Paige wasn't particularly surprised when she got home a few minutes past eight that evening and found the hole in her living-room wall gaping as widely as ever. She was, however, a bit surprised to find Marc d'Angelo sprawled across her sofa, one long leg dangling over the arm, the receiver of her phone wedged between his shoulder and his ear. He glanced up and smiled when she walked through the door, but he continued talking into the phone as though there were nothing at all unusual about his being there.

Tyler, dropping the small bag of groceries he was carrying and wriggling out of his jacket, seemed to take the intrusion in stride. "Does Marc live here now, Mommy?'' he asked, apparently unruffled by the possibility. ''Is he going to be my new daddy?''

Paige managed not to drop her grocery bag. She heard a snort of laughter from the direction of the telephone and wheeled around to glare at Marc. His expression was completely guileless, but Paige didn't miss the sparkle of devilry in his azure eyes. ''No,'' she said with icy precision. ''Mr. d'Angelo does not live here, contrary to what he seems to think. And if he doesn't get out of here and fill his rabbit hole in behind him, I'll be seriously tempted to take steps to ensure he never becomes anyone's daddy.''

Tyler frowned, struggling to sort this all out. ''But you said I'd have a new daddy one day.''

''One day,'' Paige assured him very calmly, turning her back on Marc. ''Help me carry these groceries into the kitchen, okay? Then it's off to bed. We've got a busy day tomorrow.''

''But—''

''Tyler, *please*!'' Paige gazed down at her son a bit desperately. ''It's too complicated to go into right now, but—''

''What your mother's trying to tell you,'' interrupted an all-too-familiar baritone from right behind Paige, ''is that she has to fall in love with a man before he can be your daddy.'' Marc stepped in front of Paige, smiling down at her, and slipped the bag of groceries out of her arms before she could protest. ''Isn't that right, Mrs. MacKenzie?''

''Quite right, Mr. d'Angelo,'' she snapped. ''Now, will you—''

"But, Mommy," piped up Tyler, "couldn't you fall in love with Marc and make *him* my daddy?"

"It doesn't work quite like that, short stuff." Marc's eyes held Paige's. "Although an optimist might be tempted to hold out for the possibility."

"An optimist might also be tempted to hold out for the possibility of hell freezing over, Mr. d'Angelo," Paige said in a voice low enough that Tyler couldn't hear.

Marc chuckled as he headed for the kitchen with the groceries. "I hear we're in for quite a cold spell this fall, Mrs. MacKenzie."

Paige stood there staring after him in disbelief, then snatched up the bag that Tyler had dropped. "Honey, I want you to run upstairs and get washed and into your pajamas. I'll be up in a few minutes to tuck you in, all right?"

"Can I play wif my toys for a little while?"

He gazed up at her so hopefully that Paige felt her resolve melt. "All right," she said with a laugh. "But just for a while, then it's into bed."

Tyler's eyes glowed as he bounced toward the stairs. "Can Marc come up to tuck me in, too?"

Paige felt herself stiffen slightly. "No." Tyler looked around at her and she forced herself to relax and smile. "Marc has to go home, honey. But I'll be up in a few minutes."

Tyler's small face fell with disappointment, but he nodded and started up the stairs. Watching him, Paige found herself frowning. Just what magic, she wondered, had Marc d'Angelo woven around her son?

Marc had set the bag of groceries on the counter

and was casually rummaging through it when Paige caught up to him. He gave her another one of those impossibly charming smiles. "Got anything to eat in here?"

Two

"**M**ouse poison," Paige told him succinctly, pulling the bag out of his hands.

"Don't be nasty." Marc grabbed a package of cookies off the top. "How about a cup of coffee to go with these?"

"Will you get out of here!" Paige snatched the package away from him. "Just where do you get off acting as though you own the place?"

"As a matter of fact, I nearly did." Marc calmly took the package of cookies out of her hand and tore it open. "I wanted to buy the entire house, but this side wasn't for sale when my original offer came in. When it finally went on the market a few months later, I was on a canoe trip up in Algonquin Park. By the time my real estate agent got hold of me and we worked up an offer, you'd come in with yours." He grinned at her. "You stole it right out from under my nose."

"Which makes it all right to knock down my living-room wall and just generally make yourself at home, does it?"

"The wall was a mistake." Marc offered her a cookie, and when she ignored it, he took it himself. "And I was in your living room tonight because your phone kept ringing and I thought it might be important."

"That call was for *me*?"

"Someone by the name of Daniel." He set even white teeth across the cookie and bit into it, watching her idly. "Wanted to know why you hadn't met him for lunch today."

"Oh, no!" Paige stared at him in horror. "I forgot all about it!"

"Special friend?"

"Just...a friend." Not as special a friend as Daniel would like to be, Paige thought with an inward sigh. She had kept their relationship strictly casual, but the more intent she was on keeping him at arm's length, the more intent he became on changing her mind. Frankly, he was starting to get on her nerves. And in spite of her annoyance at Marc's casual intrusion into her life, she was secretly glad he'd taken Daniel's call. The last thing she needed tonight was another one of Daniel's convoluted arguments about why she should go out with him.

"He made it sound more serious than that," Marc commented, taking another bite of the cookie.

"Wanted to know who I was, why I was answering your phone, stuff like that."

"I'd like to know who you think you are and why you're answering my phone, too," Paige muttered. "And my relationship with Daniel is none of your business." She turned away and started putting the groceries away.

There was no reply beyond a thoughtful grunt. Ignoring him, Paige stood on her toes and strained to slide a box of crackers onto the top shelf. A tanned hand came out of the air behind her, took the box and set it on the high shelf with ease. "He sounded like a jerk."

"Will you mind your own business!"

"Does Tyler like him?" Marc took a box of cake mix from her hand and set it beside the crackers.

Paige held out another box. "No. He doesn't like men at all, as a matter of fact." *Except you, apparently,* she very nearly added, catching herself just in time.

Marc gave her a quizzical look. "He's a good kid. It must be rough raising him on your own like this." He put the box up on the shelf.

"Sometimes," Paige said softly, surprised by her own candor. What was it about this aggravating man, she wondered, that made you feel he really cared? "Although I'm not really alone. My parents live here in Toronto."

"Parents can't take the place of a husband and father."

"No, they can't." She let her gaze slide away from those probing azure eyes.

"How long has it been?"

"Nearly three years. My husband was killed in a car accident."

"Tyler was just a baby."

"Fourteen months. He doesn't remember Peter, but he's old enough now to realize that other kids have fathers. And to wonder why he doesn't. I've tried to explain it to him, but…" She shrugged. "It's hard to explain death to a four-year-old."

"Harder yet to explain the intricacies of finding him another father," Marc offered with a chuckle.

Paige looked up at him sharply, then surprised herself by laughing. "Just about as hard as trying to explain it to his grandparents."

"Ahhh." Marc smiled knowingly. "The old 'We don't care if he *is* a jerk, he'll be a good husband and father' argument."

"More or less. Or, failing that, the old 'But why live by yourself when there's a perfectly good apartment above the coach house you could use?' argument."

"Complete with live-in baby-sitters."

Paige nodded thoughtfully. "I know it's hard for them to let go. To let me grow up."

"You'll always be their little girl," Marc said quietly. "When you hurt, they hurt. And they'll always try to help."

"I don't need anyone's help." Her tone was steely. She looked up at Marc defiantly and found him watching her. Flushing at the vehemence in her own voice, she gave her head a toss. "And I don't need your help, either. So if you're finished answering my phone and eating my groceries, why don't you pretend you're Alice's White Rabbit and vanish?''

Smiling, Marc helped himself to another cookie and started to stroll toward the door. ''It wasn't the White Rabbit that vanished; it was the Cheshire Cat. He just smiled and...disappeared.'' And with that he, too, smiled and disappeared.

The kitchen seemed very empty, and Paige looked around her with a sigh. She always hated the nights. During the day she was too busy to worry, but in the evenings, after Tyler had gone to bed, the stillness seemed to close around her, magnifying every doubt, every fear. It was always then when she found herself tempted to just give up this silly dream of running her own business.

That's what her father called it. ''Paige, this silly dream of yours is admirable,'' he'd tell her. ''But face it, princess, it's impractical. Why put yourself and Tyler through all this when you don't have to? Move back home. You can have all the independence you want right here.''

Paige smiled wearily. She took a cookie out of the open package and wandered into the dining room, at the back of the house. Munching it thoughtfully, she stood in front of the sliding glass patio doors and stared out across the raised wooden deck that took up most of the tiny backyard. The towering chestnut trees lining the back lane blotted out most of the evening sky. They seemed to be decorated for some gala event, their huge arching canopies bedecked with glowing white candle-shaped blossoms. But Paige hardly noticed their beauty. Instead, she was thinking about Cabbages and Kings.

Because Cabbages and Kings, an upscale little restaurant in the trendy, recently renovated area of downtown Toronto called Cabbagetown, could be the break she needed. The two young owners had shown considerable interest when she'd suggested they carry her preserves. She had an appointment with them tomorrow morning to talk about it further and was taking along samples of her ginger chutney and marmalade. Cabbages and Kings catered to the people who mattered in Toronto. And one never knew who might taste her ginger chutney and take a liking to it.

All she *did* know, Paige thought gloomily, was that if she didn't get a break soon, she was going to be in serious trouble. Until now, she'd been selling her small pots of jam and relishes at the tiny gourmet and specialty shops in the neighborhood. They sold well and were bringing in a steady income, but after the initial euphoria of actually selling her products had worn off, she'd realized an unpleasant truth: They didn't bring in enough money to live on. She had to expand her market, and that meant reaching beyond the exclusive little shops in the area. She had to find some way to make GingerBread Preserves a familiar name. One way to do that was to have her products appear on the tables of some of Toronto's finest restaurants, and that's where Cabbages and Kings came in.

And if she failed? That was simple. If she failed, she'd have to accept her father's offer of either financial help or a job with his investment consulting firm.

The offers were sincere, made with her welfare and that of his only grandson in mind, but both held the ultimate pitfall: She'd be expected to move back into the big family house up in Rosedale, one of Toronto's wealthiest neighborhoods. Just like the helpless little girl she sometimes felt like. Back to Daddy.

No. Paige straightened, mouth set in a firm, determined line. Not this time! This time she was going to make it on her own. She wasn't a child anymore, running home to her parents when her dreams fell apart unexpectedly. She was a twenty-seven-year-old woman and a mother, and it was darned well time she started acting like it.

She turned and walked back into the kitchen. She wrenched open the refrigerator door, pulled out the big bowls of washed, sliced apricots and set them on the counter. Enough for twelve jars of ginger apricot jam. She'd be up half the night making it, as usual, but there was no avoiding that. Guiltily, she thought of Tyler. He'd be in bed by now, waiting patiently for her to come up and read him a bedtime story. She looked at the bowls of fruit, then at the clock. She'd dash up right now and tuck him in, but the story would have to wait, she decided as she reached for her apron. Maybe tomorrow night...

It was the sun that wakened Paige the next morning. It poured through the windows and across the bed as warm as melted butter, and she lay there listening sleepily to the clamor of sparrows outside the bedroom window. She opened one eye and peered at the clock.

Nine-thirty! Paige sat up with a gasp, staring at the clock in utter disbelief. "Oh, no! I forgot to set the alarm!"

She was on her feet in the next instant, trying to remember when she was supposed to be down at Cabbages and Kings. A scant two hours from now— enough time if everything went smoothly. She'd shower before getting Tyler up, then she could dress while he was eating breakfast. That would give her just enough time to drop him off with her mother before racing back down to the restaurant with the jam, then...

Possibilities and options whirled through her mind as she hurried down the hall toward Tyler's bedroom. Preoccupied with the logistical problems of her morning, she didn't see the patch of water-soaked carpet until she'd set one bare foot right in the middle of it. Icy water welled up between her toes and she gave a gasp and leaped back, staring at the carpet in surprise. Then, groaning, she looked up at the skylight. It was fogged with condensation, and discolored patches stained the wooden frame where rainwater had come in during the night's thunderstorm. She swore at it angrily. How could it betray her like that! And if it *had* to leak, why couldn't it wait for a few months until she had the money to repair it?

Shoulders slumping, she took a couple of bath towels from the linen closet and laid them across the wet patch of carpeting, pressing them down into the wet pile to soak up as much water as possible. Just terrific. This damned old house was full of surprises. Rarely a day went by that it didn't reveal another of its little quirks.

Swearing under her breath, she pushed open the bathroom door. The water was steaming hot, for a change. Smiling at this rare luxury, Paige deliberately took her time in the shower, deciding the few stolen minutes wouldn't make her any more late. She soaped herself thoroughly from head to toe, then stood under the sluicing water as she worked up a good lather with the shampoo. Maybe she wouldn't have to have the entire plumbing system replaced after all, she mused. Maybe it would hold together until summer.

"Hey, Marco. You sure this is the right one?" Carmine Agostini gazed mistrustfully at the Chinese puzzle of piping above his head. "We cut the wrong one, we're in big trouble."

"It's the right one," Marc murmured absently. He was staring down at the faded blueprint he'd spread out on the dusty basement floor, but he was thinking of Paige. Of her golden brown eyes, like agate one moment and as soft and warm as melted chocolate the next. Of the silken curve of her throat and shoulder...

"Okay," Carmine sighed. He slid the welder's mask down and lit the torch. When it spat blue fire, he adjusted the flame expertly. "But if we cut the wrong one, my friend, you're going to have one very mad lady next door."

"Yeah," Marc murmured dreamily. "Yeah, go ahead."

He was so immersed in his thoughts that he didn't

even realize that Carmine had started cutting into the pipe until he heard a startled yell. He looked up, then leaped to his feet and raced across the basement to the water shutoff valve. "What the hell are you doing?" he shouted over his shoulder as he cranked the valve closed. The spout of water deluging Carmine slowed to a trickle, leaving him soaked to the skin and sputtering furiously in Italian.

"What am *I* doing?" he finally got out. "What're *you* doing, you mean! You say you know which pipe to cut. You say go ahead. Then...blooey! Niagara Falls!" Muttering ferociously to himself, Carmine shut the torch off and tossed it aside. The heavy mask followed.

"Oh, hell," sighed Marc wearily. "I guess we'd better go next door and sort all this out before Paige finds out we've just cut her water off."

Paige gave a squeak of dismay when the water cut off abruptly. She wiped shampoo out of her eyes and stared stupidly at the faucet, then bent down and turned it experimentally. Nothing. Shampoo and soap dripped into the tub. "I don't *believe* this!" She wiggled the faucet angrily, then turned it off, back on again. It yielded nothing but a solitary drop of rusty water. She swore enthusiastically as shampoo ran into her eyes and made them sting. She stepped out of the tub and wrapped a big towel around herself, wiping her eyes with one corner as she pulled the bathroom door open. "I swear I'll have the whole thing torn out nut by bolt, and—*oh*!" She went rigid with surprise, clutching the towel.

A small, dark-eyed man stepped by her with a nod of greeting, not even seeming to notice that she was clad in only a towel and soapy water. He set down the huge toolbox and started to unscrew the access panel to the tub's piping. "Gino, the plumber," he said matter-of-factly. "Gino Agostini. I'm working for Marc d'Angelo."

"Somehow," Paige told him very calmly, "that doesn't surprise me at all." Who else, she thought as she stalked down the stairs, would be behind this but Marc d'Angelo?

The thought occurred to Paige halfway down the basement stairs that it might have been a good idea if she'd stopped to get dressed first. But it was too late now. She hesitated at the bottom of the steps and looked around distastefully. This was the only part of Chestnut Manor she could have happily done without. It was dark and clammy and filled with cobwebs and small scurrying things that avoided the light. Especially uninviting was the far end, where the old hot-water boiler and its attending tangle of pipes and valves lurked in deep shadows. And that was exactly where the trouble—and whoever was causing it—lay. Wrinkling her nose, she strode across the basement, leaving a trail of wet footprints and shampoo.

Three men squatted around the boiler in a semicircle, looking like pagan priests squatting around some bloated and faintly obscene deity. She wouldn't have been surprised had they started chanting and waving prayer wheels at the thing.

It was only when she got up to them that she realized the three men were really two men and a boy.

Tyler squatted on his heels between Marc and the other man, his pajamas filthy, cobwebs and dirt clinging to his tousled hair. He was clutching the handle of a wrench that probably weighed more than he did, and he watched Marc raptly.

"Tyler!" Paige stared at her son in disbelief. "What on earth have you been doing?"

The three of them started badly and turned; three pairs of eyes widened as they took in her soaking hair and towel. "Uh-oh," said the stranger softly.

"Hi, Mommy!" Tyler leaped to his feet. His dirty face glowed with excitement. "Guess what! Marc's lettin' me help him, an' Carmine says I'm the best plumber he's ever seen, an'—"

"Tyler, I've told you a hundred times to stay away from this boiler. It's much too dangerous for you to—"

"We've been keeping an eye on him," Marc put in quietly. "He heard us and came down to investigate. I figured it would keep him quiet while you were trying to sleep in."

"I wasn't supposed to be sleeping in!" Paige knew it was hardly Marc's fault she'd forgotten to set the alarm, but at the moment she didn't care how irrational her anger was. "And just what," she added furiously, "have you done to my water?"

He winced. "I'm, uh, sorry about that."

"I don't care how sorry you are. I just want my water turned back on!"

"We're trying." He nodded toward the other man. "This is Carmine Agostini, by the way. His brother Gino's upstairs looking for—".

"We've met," Paige said succinctly. "Now would you like to tell me why *your* plumbers have turned off *my* water?"

"God knows," Marc muttered, glaring at the boiler. His bare shoulders and torso were covered with dirt and cobwebs, and Paige realized that he'd been crawling around under it. She gave a little shudder. "I'm installing a gas furnace and overhauling the entire plumbing system on my side. But this old boiler once supplied all the hot water and heating steam for the entire house, and some of the piping is still common." He nodded toward the brick wall dividing his side of the basement from hers, and the tangle of pipes and wiring running through it. "The problem is the whole system's like a jigsaw puzzle. We can't tell from my side what's still connected and what isn't. And obviously the pipe we just cut into *is*."

"If you'd hire professionals instead of getting your friends to do it, you wouldn't have this problem," Paige pointed out, refusing to be mollified that easily.

It took a lot of effort, but Marc managed not to smile. She was mad now; if she thought he was laughing at her, she'd go up like a Chinese rocket. "Agostini Plumbing is one of the best in the business," he told her patiently. "But by the look of it, this system was designed and installed by the same engineers who outfitted Noah. I don't need a plumber; I need an archaeologist."

That stopped her. She sputtered a few words of protest, then settled for glowering at him as though he were personally responsible for the house's shortcomings. He grinned, wondering if she had even the slightest idea of how seductive she looked in that towel, bare shoulders and throat dewed with water, wet hair tousled and still frothy with shampoo. He found himself unable to stop the next images from forming: of her *in* the shower, deliciously naked, soapy water cascading over her silken skin, firm breasts lifting as she raised her arms to rinse her hair...

The image was a little too vivid. Marc's stomach muscles pulled taut, and he took a deep breath and forced himself to think about something else—how he was going to get that wall upstairs repaired, for instance—until he was certain his body wasn't going to betray those unexpected longings and embarrass him thoroughly. She had good reason to be upset, he had to admit. He had no business fooling around with this mess without having talked it over with her first. He was just too impatient; that was the problem. He wasn't used to needing anyone's permission to do something; he'd spent the last sixteen years doing things *his* way, according to *his* schedules and plans.

He sighed inwardly. "We'll get it fixed, Paige. Even if we have to resort to an exorcist and an offering of goat entrails. Which," he added with a glowering look at the boiler, "is about the only thing we *haven't* tried."

"If it isn't working in ten minutes," Paige advised him darkly, "I'm going to resort to human sacrifice. And *your* entrails are going to be in serious jeopardy, mister." Carmine gave a delighted chuckle. He sobered when Paige glared at him.

"An hour," Marc promised, ignoring Carmine's

astonished look. "Why don't you go over to my place and wash that shampoo out of your hair? The water's still on over there."

"It would be." She grabbed Tyler's grubby hand and wheeled away. "One hour. A moment more, and I come down here looking for blood." She glanced over her shoulder. *"Anyone's."*

"Hey!" Marc's voice brought her up short. She stopped, one foot on the bottom step, and turned to glare at him. "You got a call this morning from Sean and DiCarlo over at Cabbages and Kings. They wondered if you could come in a half hour early this morning." Her eyes widened with horror, and Marc smiled reassuringly. "Don't worry. I told them it wasn't convenient. So we settled on two this afternoon. That okay?"

"You…what?" Her eyes grew even wider.

"I checked your appointment book by the phone. You didn't have anything at two except a shampoo and trim at Sylvio's. I figured your meeting with Cabbages was more important than a haircut, so I called Sylvio and rebooked your appointment for next week. Tuesday, I think. I wrote it down for you."

"I don't believe this!" She stared at him in helpless anger. "Is there no part of my life sacred to you? Maybe I should just hire you as my social secretary."

Marc smiled. "Just trying to help. You looked a little frazzled around the edges when I left here last night. I figured you needed the sleep more than you needed the aggravation. If it had been important, I'd have called you."

"Thank you," she told him with cutting pleasantness, her dark eyes flashing. "Now do me another favor—don't *do* me any more favors. You are the prime cause of the frazzle around my edges, Mr. d'Angelo. And you're right. I *don't* need any more aggravation in my life." She turned and stalked up the stairs.

The towel did more to emphasize than conceal her long slender legs and the curve of her upper thighs. Seeing Marc watching her, Carmine gave a knowing chuckle beside him and he turned away, flushing. "Let's get to work," he growled. "You go back to my side and start tagging those pipes. I'll be over as soon as I finish sorting this wiring out."

You're behaving like a randy teenager, Marc told himself disgustedly as he watched Carmine hurry up the stairs. Besides, he added with a touch of philosophical gloominess, she was probably already involved with someone. He could be upstairs right now, sprawled out in her bed still sound asleep, pleasantly exhausted by a night's worth of excesses. Daniel whatever-the-hell-his-name-was, for instance. Although he hadn't sounded like the all-night type. And if Paige knew her son didn't like the jerk, surely she wouldn't let him stay over till morning.

Marc caught the direction of his thoughts and gave his head an annoyed shake. He'd met the woman all of twenty-four hours ago, and he'd already spent the better part of a day and an entire night thinking about her, his dreams so erotic and vivid he'd awakened aching with the wanting of her. And now he was criticizing a lover who might not even exist. Old age, he chided himself.

It was nearly half an hour later when he heard something hit the counter upstairs with a crash. Marc winced when whatever it was hit the floor even more loudly. He drew in a deep breath and was about to ease himself in behind the boiler when Paige's startled exclamation stopped him. It was followed by a horrendous clatter of breaking dishes, then Tyler's wail of fear.

Marc was across the basement and up the stairs in ten long strides. He threw the door into the kitchen open and ducked instinctively as something flew by his head. The heavy china meat platter hit the floor and exploded into a dozen pieces, followed by a handful of smaller plates as the upper section of kitchen cabinetry pulled the rest of the way off the wall, spilling its contents noisily around Paige. Pinned against the stove, she was trying desperately to hold the cabinet up, catch falling plates and keep from being crushed at the same time.

"Help!" she sputtered unnecessarily, fending off a fresh avalanche of dishes. "Look out—the plates! Tyler, get back!"

Marc caught the spilling plates handily, managing to save all but one. He placed them on the counter, then turned and scooped up Tyler, who was standing wide-eyed and whimpering with shock. He deposited the frightened boy in the living room, where he was well out of range of falling dishes and broken glass, and pointed a stern finger at him. "Stay put!"

Tyler nodded, hugging his yellow blanket desperately, and Marc paused long enough to ruffle the boy's hair reassuringly before turning back to the kitchen. He grabbed the cabinet in both hands and shoved it with all his strength. "Get out from under there! Move!"

"But my dishes!" Paige wailed, grabbing a covered sugar bowl as it tipped toward her. The creamer followed, and she snatched it out of midair, cradling them both as she tried to save a stack of dessert bowls.

"Forget the dishes!" Marc ducked as a butter dish skated across the steeply sloping shelf and flew out at him. It hit his shoulder and bounced toward Paige, who fielded it deftly and set it safely to one side. "Paige…!"

"Just hang on to it for a minute," she pleaded, snatching a handful of dinner plates as they shot toward her. She managed to save them but had to watch helplessly as an entire shelf of wineglasses cascaded out onto the floor and shattered. "The teapot," she cried in utter anguish. "Oh, no, that's my great-grandmother's teapot!"

Instinctively, Marc let go of the cupboard with one hand and tidily caught the teapot as it sailed by him. Paige gave a little gasp of relief and took it from him tenderly, her face radiant as she gazed at the treasured piece. It could have been part of the crown jewels, Marc thought with amusement, watching her as she carefully set it down, well out of danger from falling debris or jostling elbows.

She turned just then and her eyes met his squarely, russet depths glowing with gratitude, and Marc felt something inside tighten so sharply that his breath caught. She smiled at him then, the corners of that deliciously kissable mouth tipping up almost shyly, and Marc could have sworn he felt the universe tremble just ever so slightly. His shoulder muscles were screaming with the effort of holding the cupboard up, but he ignored the pain; the expression on that small, heart-shaped face was worth every moment of agony. He'd hang on to this damned thing for the rest of eternity if it meant another one of those marvelous smiles.

"Hey, Marco? You in there?" a man called from the living room.

Marc ignored the distant voice, willing it to go away, content simply to stand there and gaze into the warm eyes that still held his, so close he could see flecks of amber and green in them. The voice came again, muttering querulously in Italian this time, and her marvelous brown eyes blinked, growing puzzled.

Marc sighed. "In here," he called in resignation. "And I could use a hand."

Footsteps crunched through crumbled brick and mortar. There was another mutter of Italian, then a stocky figure stepped into the kitchen. The older man gazed at the scene in amazement, taking in the piles of broken china, Paige's look of helpless desperation, Marc's straining body, half hidden by the fallen cupboard.

"What you doing?" he demanded, setting two large, dusty hands on his hips, the better to survey the damage.

"Posing for an ad in *Body Builder's Gazette*, Pop," Marc shot back with exaggerated calm. His shoulder felt as if it were afire. "What does it look like I'm doing?"

"Looks like you're ruining this lady's home, that's what it looks like," came the prompt reply. "You couldn't take the dishes out before pulling off the cupboard? Most people, they take the dishes out first."

"Pop!" Marc shifted his weight, trying to ease the strain on his shoulder. "Could we save the handyman's lecture for *after* we get this thing off me? It's heavy as hell."

"Don't swear in front of the lady," his father chided him. Then he leaned over to shout through the doorway. "Gregorio! In here! Your brother, he made a mess like you wouldn't believe."

Marc groaned. He could hear heavy footsteps crunching through what was left of Paige's living room wall, then an astonished oath followed by a whoop of laughter. Marc's younger brother appeared in the kitchen door, grinning. "Holy—!" He saw Paige just then and caught himself in time, his grin widening. "My brother do that to your wall?" His eyes twinkled. "Old Marco really did it this time, hey, Pop?"

"You watch your mouth. Your brother, he's doing okay."

"Sorry, Pop." Completely unabashed, Greg turned every megawatt of smile on Paige, who was still standing there looking a little stunned. "Pop and me, we're helping Marc renovate his house. My name's Greg. Greg d'Angelo."

Marc gritted his teeth as his brother, bare-chested

and clad like him in only blue jeans and construction boots, sucked in his already flat stomach and threw out his broad chest a bit further. Only seventeen, he was just starting to become aware of the effect that six feet of tanned muscle, blue eyes and boyish good looks had on women.

"Would it be anywhere in the realm of possibility," Marc asked very reasonably, "for me to get some help over here?"

Greg looked around, taking in the scene with interest. "Wouldn't it have been easier to take the dishes out first?"

"Help your brother," his father suggested smoothly, cutting off Marc's enraged bellow.

"Would the mop work?" All three of them looked at her, and Paige gestured toward the cupboard. "The mop. Could we use it to prop up the cupboard temporarily?"

"It's flimsy," Marc said, "but let's give it a try. Ram it between the two—"

But she was way ahead of him and had already levered the mop between the cabinet he and Greg were holding and the ones on the opposite side of the narrow kitchen.

He wet his lips. "Okay, Greg, let it go. Stand well back—if that handle breaks, it'll splinter like shrapnel." Marc waited for Greg to get clear, then he eased his grip on the cupboard. The mop bowed dangerously as it took the weight of the cabinet, but it held. Marc backed from between the cabinets as though sidestepping live artillery. Broken glass crunched beneath his heavy work boots, and he looked down at

Paige's bare feet. "Don't move," he ordered. She gave him a startled look, clearly not understanding. "Glass," he said simply, settling his hands around her waist. "Broken glass."

She'd replaced the towel with an oversized man's shirt, and Marc swore he could feel the silken texture of her skin right through the light fabric. She gasped as he lifted her gently into the air, but she didn't struggle. She was as light as thistledown and deliciously warm and soft in his hands, her hair and skin scented with soap and sunshine.

He set her down in the archway leading to the living room and drew his hands from her slowly. "Don't walk around here without a pair of shoes," he told her gruffly, his hands still tingling from the warmth of her. Wanting to touch her again, even briefly, he took her by the arm and drew her away from the kitchen, nodding toward the half-collapsed cupboard. "Don't even breathe heavily, and maybe that mop will hold until I can get back in here with something more solid. Better yet, get out of here altogether. If that handle gives, the cabinet will come down like a trapdoor. And it won't come down clean. It'll twist and bounce as it rips the rest of the way free, and you could get hurt."

She looked slightly shell-shocked as she let him lead her out, eyes very large and dark in her pale face. Poor kid, he found himself thinking. Must have scared the hell out of her, reaching up to get a bowl and having the whole cupboard come down on top of her.

He found himself suddenly wanting to cradle her against him, to breathe in the sweet scent of her hair again, to feel the pliant warmth of her. He shook himself free of the image and settled instead on touching her shoulder lightly. "Are you hurt?"

"No. It just startled the daylights out of me." She looked up at him and smiled that marvelous smile again, and Marc felt a band tighten around his chest. "Thank you."

"Hey, Marc, you want me to—"

"You come and help me," his father said firmly, taking the younger man by the arm and tugging him toward the door. "Marco, you think you can handle this by yourself?"

There was a hint of mischief in his father's voice and eyes, and Marc grinned. "I think I can handle it, Pop. Thanks."

"My name is Vincenzo d'Angelo," his father said to Paige, extending his hand with a broad smile. "My boy here, he's a pretty good carpenter." He gave Marc a fatherly slap on the shoulder. "He's spent the last sixteen years forgetting everything I teach him, but he's learning again. He's a good boy."

"I can handle it, Pop," Marc said dryly. "See you later."

His father and Greg left, grinning like bandits, and Marc glanced around at Paige. She was rooting around in the cupboard by the door leading to the basement, and after a moment she pulled out a pair of sneakers and put them on. One very cool lady, he decided approvingly. He was thinking about telling her exactly that, as a matter of fact, when she calmly stepped by him.

"Excuse me. I have to get my jam."

It took him so by surprise that he just stood there gaping at her. It was only when she actually started to duck under the bowed mop handle that he was galvanized into action. "Hey!" He pounced toward her. He had the momentary sensation of silken skin under his fingertips; then he was grasping thin air and she was well beyond his reach.

Three

———

"**W**hat the hell do you think you're doing?" Marc bellowed in astonishment. "Get out of there! If this mop gives, the cupboard's going to come down and squash you flat!"

"I've got to get my jam," Paige repeated firmly. "If these jars get broken, being squashed flat by a renegade kitchen cupboard will be the least of my problems."

"Damn it, what—?" But Marc swallowed the rest of it and settled for a grumbled curse instead as Paige pulled the plastic dish drainer out from under the sink, apparently oblivious to the fact that the cupboard above her head could come down on top of her at any instant. He braced his palms against the cabinet. "Hurry up."

Using the drainer as a makeshift basket, Paige

started filling it with the small neatly labeled jars of golden preserves lined up along the sink. "In a minute," she replied serenely, not paying the slightest heed to the urgency in his voice. She lifted the jars delicately, as though each contained some rare and magical elixir.

"What the hell's in those?" Marc grumbled. "Liquid gold?" He was starting to wish he'd stayed in bed this morning. Somehow all this heroic stuff looked a lot easier in the movies.

"Just about," Paige murmured, clearly too preoccupied with her little jars to be impressed by any heroics going on around her.

Although it would be nice, he decided as he gazed down at the top of her sleekly shining head, if she could at least *pretend* to listen to what he had to say. "I've heard about food addictions, but this is ridiculous," he grumbled. "Leave the rest of them. I'll buy you a case from the grocery store."

She gave him a look of sublime disgust. "This is not just jam; this is *my* jam. My own special recipe. It's what pays the mortgage on this house." Finally the last jar joined its companions and she lifted the drainer gently. She stepped by him. "And if the thrill of playing Hercules is starting to pall, you can leave, you know. I was managing quite well on my own before you decided to knock my wall down and take over my life."

He was tempted, for a fraction of a second, to let the whole cupboard drop then and there. But he didn't. He satisfied himself by muttering a ferocious oath under his breath that earned him another frosty glare, and eased himself clear of the cabinet. "Take your little pots and get out of this kitchen," he told her flatly. "Then stay out until I get back to fix that cupboard."

He distinctly heard her breath suck in as she wheeled around to face him. There was enough heat in her eyes to char brick, and he watched as she fought to control herself. He thought for one tension-filled moment that she was going to drop that precious basket of jam and explode with sheer fury. Then, to his satisfaction, she seemed to weigh her options and realize that he was right. She nodded once, nostrils flaring like a racehorse at the starting gate. "Then go," she advised him. "And while you're running around fixing things, don't forget my water's still off."

He felt his own temper starting to rise and caught it firmly, not saying a word as he turned and strode across the living room to the pile of bricks and mortar still scattered across the floor. Beelzebub, he thought again. The old cat's golden eyes blazed with the same subdued heat when he was crossed. He found himself smiling. Just what was it about Paige MacKenzie, he wondered as he slipped through the hole into his own living room, that made him feel as dizzy and disoriented as if he'd just stepped off a roller coaster?

What was it about Marc d'Angelo, Paige found herself wondering, that made her feel like a tongue-tied teenager? He wasn't even particularly good-looking, although he had that rugged, roughneck sort of masculine appeal that made women look twice. But that alone shouldn't have done it. No, it had more to do with the matter-of-fact way he'd stepped through that wall and into her life yesterday without even so much as a murmur of apology. He had the calm self-assurance of someone who knew exactly what he was doing and where he was going and hadn't a doubt from dawn to dusk about the rightness of his life. Someone, Paige thought with an inward sigh, a bit like her father.

And that was exactly what she didn't need right now: another Harrington J. Pricefield trying to run her life.

The traitorous thought gave Paige a twinge of guilt, and she sighed again, aloud this time. She smiled at Tyler, who had apparently recovered from his fright and was gazing yearningly at the hole in the wall. "Hungry?"

Tyler shook his head without looking at her, watching the hole with rapt anticipation as though expecting Alice's white rabbit—or Marc d'Angelo—to pop through at any instant. He gave his dusty pajama bottoms an absent hitch as they threatened to slide down, and Paige's smile widened. They were faded almost white from countless washings and the elastic in the waistband had given out months ago, but Tyler flatly refused to let her toss them out. Like the tattered yellow blanket he lugged around all day, the pajamas were old friends, and Paige knew they gave him some small sense of security in a bewildering world where fathers left without saying goodbye and mothers cried all night.

"Well, honey, it's getting late. And I have a lot to

do today. Grandma's expecting us in about an hour, so run upstairs and wash while I make breakfast."

"You going out today?" Tyler looked at her unhappily, hugging the blanket a little tighter. "Again?"

As always, the disappointment in his voice tore at Paige like a physical pain. She slipped her arms around him and hugged him, resting her cheek against his corn-silk hair. "I have to, honey. I have to buy more jars and pick up those new labels I ordered, then drop by the printer to look at a sample of the advertising brochures I designed. *And* I have to deliver this jam to the Cabbages and Kings restaurant and give them the best sales pitch of my life!"

"They could come here," Tyler offered hopefully.

Paige kissed the top of his head. "It doesn't work like that, Tyler. I'm trying to convince them to buy my jams regularly, so I have to go to them. But I won't be late. And your grandma said she'd take you down to the petting zoo at Riverdale Farm. You like going there, don't you?"

"I guess so," Tyler replied, not sounding very convinced. "But I'd rather go with *you*."

Paige gave him an extra hug. "I know, sweetheart. And I'd give anything in the world to be able to take you. But if I don't get some major markets for my jam and compotes pretty fast, we're going to be out on the welfare line."

"You're *never* home," Tyler said, his lower lip starting to jut out. He wriggled free of her grasp and looked up at her accusingly. "Ever since we moved here. I hate this house. I want to go back to the other house."

"Tyler, this is our home now." Paige heard the slight edge of impatience in her voice and swallowed it. Tyler was too young to understand the memories that first house held for her, memories of the woman she'd been back then. But his unhappiness still hurt. It was as though he were criticizing not only her decisions but *her*, the multifaceted person she'd become these past three years: mother, businesswoman, income earner.

She forced herself to smile with a cheeriness she didn't feel. "That house belongs to those other people now. Remember the family with the little boy your age who bought it? You wouldn't want to take his home away from him, would you? Where would he live?"

"He could live with *his* grandma," Tyler shot back with perfect logic. His lip started to tremble, and Paige knew from sad experience that if she didn't act fast, there was going to be a torrent of tears at any instant.

"Look, Tyler," she said softly, sitting down on the step beside him and putting her hands on his shoulders. "I know this isn't easy, but you're going to have to trust me, okay? I know I'm not spending as much time with you as either of us would like, and I know you're getting tired of being passed back and forth between your grandparents' house and here. But sometimes we have to do things we don't like." It was a stupid argument to use on a four-year-old, Paige knew. She was pretty sick of it herself, as a matter of fact, but the truth was that she couldn't think of anything else to tell him.

Despairingly she watched a tear slide down Tyler's cheek. "Tyler, we've been through this before," she told him firmly. Why couldn't he understand? Why couldn't he see that she was doing the best she could with what she had? "Until GingerBread Preserves catches on and starts selling itself, I'm going to be very, very busy, and that's all there is to it. I don't like it either. It doesn't mean I don't love you just as much as I always did. It just means that I think you're a big enough boy now that you can help me by accepting it for a while longer."

"I'm *not* a big boy!" Tyler wailed through a gush of tears, stamping one bare foot ineffectually on the carpeted stair. "I'm just a little boy, an' I don't ever want to be a big boy if...if..." The rest was lost under a new flood of tears.

"Tyler, please!" Paige felt desperately close to tears herself. "You have to understand that—"

"Say, short stuff, do you think you could give me a hand here?" The voice startled then both badly. Tyler swallowed a sob and wiped his cheek with one pudgy fist as Marc ducked through the hole in the wall. Grinning lazily, he squatted beside them and held out a carpenter's level. "Think you can hold this for me for a while? I've got more than I can handle."

Tyler stared at the level, then at Marc. "Me?"

"Yeah, you," Marc assured him with a chuckle. "I wasn't much older than you are now when my father put me to work carrying tools and picking up stray nails. Hang around me for a couple of weeks, and I'll make a first-rate carpenter out of you.''

Tyler's eyes widened with pride, tears already drying. He took the level reverently in both hands and giggled as the bubble slid to one end of the inset glass tube.

Marc leaned toward him, pointing at the tube with a dusty finger. ''See those two lines? The trick is to keep the bubble balanced right between them. Think you can do that?''

Tyler nodded vigorously, tongue caught between his teeth as he concentrated intently on keeping the level steady.

Paige smiled gratefully at her neighbor over the top of Tyler's head. ''Thank you.''

''Any time.'' Marc unfolded to his feet, shifting the hammer and length of lumber he was carrying to his other hand. He ruffled Tyler's hair, then gazed down at Paige. ''Has anyone ever told you the effect that smile of yours has on a man?'' he asked softly. And then, before Paige could get her startled wits together to answer, he turned away and strode toward the kitchen.

It took Paige twice as long as it usually did to get Tyler washed and dressed. Part of the problem was persuading him to put the level down long enough to scrub his face and brush his teeth, and part of it was his sudden determination to dress himself without any help whatsoever from his mother, thank you very much. They had a minor confrontation over shoes— Paige thought he needed them, and Tyler thought otherwise—and then a more serious one over making his

bed that ended with him throwing a tantrum and
Paige, patience gone, applying a firm smack to his
bottom.

The resulting howls of surprised outrage echoed
through the house, and Paige heard the steady hammering in the kitchen falter and then stop. Just keep
working, Paige advised her neighbor with silent fury
as she closed Tyler's door quietly and walked down
to the master bedroom. After all, he was the reason
behind Tyler's sudden rebelliousness this morning.

She was already regretting losing her patience with
Tyler. It wasn't his fault. He was a normal, curious
little boy, and what four-year-old could concentrate
on washing his face and making his bed when there
were infinitely more interesting things going on down
in the kitchen?

She smiled fondly as the indignant howls issuing
from Tyler's bedroom grew fainter until all she could
hear was an occasional sob. He'd come out in a few
minutes seeking the reassuring hug and kiss he knew
were always there, then the two of them would go
down for breakfast, anger behind them. If there was
any kitchen left to have breakfast in, she thought,
wincing at an extra-loud spate of hammering from
downstairs. It sounded as though d'Angelo was finishing what rotten wood and gravity had started.

She couldn't say she hadn't been warned. MaryAnn
Meadows, the real estate agent who had sold her the
house, had told her that the old place probably needed
a lot more work than it showed. Paige smiled to herself. The warning hadn't done the slightest bit of
good, of course. She'd fallen in love with Chestnut

Manor the instant she'd seen it. It had once been a single home, a massive brick Georgian mansion with mullioned windows and twelve-foot ceilings trimmed with intricate moldings and even a tower complete with merlons and bow slits.

The original double entrance doors had been left intact, complete with their huge panes of etched glass and hand-carved mahogany panels. The small foyer had been decorated with rubbed oak and old brick, and the two inside doors that angled off to either side, each leading to its own half of the house, were solid beveled glass, etched for privacy and set off by brass carriage lamps.

Unfortunately, on Paige's side, the splendor and elegance had ended there. The inside had been hastily finished for resale and, although livable, certainly didn't measure up to the promise outside. But Paige hadn't cared. She'd known at once that she had to have the house, even if it meant mortgaging her very soul.

It hadn't quite taken her soul, but it had come close. There had been offers and counteroffers for the house, creative financial trade-offs and much wheeling and dealing between real estate agents and bankers and assorted lawyers. Then, after a nerve-racking weekend during which she was certain she'd lost it—to none other than Marc d'Angelo, she now realized—the house had become hers.

And that's when the panic had set in. The house needed work, and lots of it. She had a four-year-old son to care for, no money, no real job, and no prospects of one. She had little business training and less

experience. All she did have was a dream called
GingerBread Preserves.

Paige smiled again, a trifle ruefully. It wasn't long
before hard, cold reality had set in. She'd had a lot
of unpleasant surprises during the past three months.
And she'd weathered all of them, each failure and
disappointment simply tempering the single-minded
determination that had gotten her this far.

This far. Paige drew in a deep. unsteady breath, her
stomach tying itself in a painful knot at just the
thought of today's meeting. She opened her tiny
closet and stood contemplating the contents for a moment, then sighed and took out her rust wool skirt and
the coppery silk blouse that went so well with it.
There wasn't a lot of choice. Her wardrobe had been
the first thing to suffer after Peter's death. She'd put
every penny toward paying off the mountain of debts
he'd left, not buying pretty clothes.

Paige was just pulling on her teddy when she heard
Tyler's bedroom door open. "I'm in here, honey."
There was no answer. Sliding the straps over her
shoulders, she peeked around the bedroom door. Tyler was standing at the top of the stairs, the yellow
blanket clutched in one hand and the level in the
other. He looked up at her, his small face still flushed
with tears.

"I'm going downstairs," he told her with a sniff,
eyes still bright with indignation at his unfair treat-
ment.

Paige pulled on the silk blouse, hiding her smile
from him, and nodded seriously. "That's fine. But
there's broken glass all over the kitchen floor, so be

very careful. And please stay out of Mr. d'Angelo's way, all right? I'll be down in a couple of minutes to fix your breakfast.''

"Don't need to fix my breakfast," Tyler declared haughtily, starting down the stairs. "I can fix breakfast my own self."

Paige had to bite her lip to keep from laughing out loud, finding her eyes unexpectedly filling with tears at the same time. Thank you, Tyler James Mac-Kenzie, she whispered silently, for keeping me sane in a world that sometimes goes a little mad! He was the one joyful reminder that she was a mature and responsible adult now, not the little girl her father still wanted her to be.

She blinked her eyes clear and pulled the elastic band out of her hair. Unbound, it spilled around her shoulders and she reached for a brush with a sigh. If she was such a responsible adult, she asked herself, why did she feel like a scared little kid so much of the time?

Even as he started up the stairs to the second floor, Marc knew he had absolutely no business wandering around Page MacKenzie's house. But the truth was that he seriously doubted that she'd invite him to do so, and he badly wanted to see what it looked like.

This old house was fast becoming an obsession, he told himself gloomily as he let Tyler lead him up the stairs. It was bad enough that he'd knocked a hole in Paige's living-room wall. Now he was lying to her son about wanting to use the bathroom just to get a peek at the upstairs of a house that would never be his.

So far, he wasn't very impressed. Like the downstairs, the second floor had been chopped up into small rooms that would have been claustrophobic had it not been for the skylight. There was a semicircular landing at the top of the stairs, off which opened two bedrooms, the bathroom and what was probably a linen closet. The landing narrowed to skirt the open stairwell, then widened again to create another open area off which led two more doors.

Paige had turned this small foyer into a sitting room, complete with an antique love seat, a tiny carved Queen Anne side table and a reading lamp. Plants were everywhere—hanging from ceiling hooks, set on the floor in huge brass planters, tucked in every available niche and corner. Brilliant sunshine poured through the skylight now, and the entire place had a warm earthy smell that Marc found oddly appealing. You could sit up here surrounded by greenery and shut out the troubles of the world, he mused.

There was a pile of damp bath towels on the floor and Tyler looked at them curiously. Then he tipped his head back and stared at the ceiling. ''Uh-oh,'' he said with a knowledgeable sigh. ''The skybright's leakin' again,''

Marc had to grin at Tyler's delightfully descriptive word. He had his mouth open to ask Tyler about it when one of the doors behind them opened.

''Tyler, are you nearly—?''

Marc looked around. His heart gave a distinct thud when his eyes met Paige's. She looked like a million dollars! he found himself thinking in wonder. She was wearing a rust-colored skirt and a lighter rust blouse of some shimmery fabric that matched her autumn-gold eyes almost perfectly. Her thick chestnut hair gleamed with the same golden highlights and it billowed loosely around her face and shoulders. The entire effect was dazzling, and Marc realized he was gaping at her like an idiot.

He also realized that she was starting to look very uneasy under his stunned appraisal, as though she saw something in his expression that unnerved her. Not surprisingly, Marc reminded himself as he eased his weight back down onto the top stair; the effect this woman was having on him unnerved *him* a bit. He couldn't remember the last time that mere eye contact with a woman had made his blood race and set his mind spinning all sorts of wondrously vivid possibilities. "Sorry, I didn't mean to startle you," he said quite truthfully. "I just wanted to—"

"He hasta use the bafroom," Tyler put in blithely.

Some of the tension evaporated. Marc grinned and was relieved to see Paige's mouth twitch with a responding smile. "Actually," he admitted with a sheepish laugh, "that was just an excuse. I really wanted to see the rest of the house."

Paige didn't say anything. A little frown wedged itself between her brows as she contemplated both him and his request. For a moment Marc was certain that she was going to suggest, in the plainest words possible, that he leave and not come back. But to his surprise she finally nodded.

"I...guess that would be all right."

She sounded so uncertain that Marc had to smile. "No ulterior motives, I swear it. This place has fascinated me since I first set eyes on it. I've spent three months trying to figure out a way to get over to this side to have a look around. You don't mind, do you?"

She did, of course. Marc could see it in her eyes. But when she smiled, there was honest warmth there. "I know what you mean," she said with a musical laugh that made his breath catch. "And I have to admit that I've been just as curious about *your* side."

"Then I'll have to give you a guided tour," Marc said with a chuckle, stepping back up onto the landing again. He nodded toward the closed doors. "Bedrooms?"

"Yes. Look, if you want."

Marc did, stepping briefly into first one small bedroom, then the other, nodding thoughtfully.

"I think this was all one room at one time." She sounded nearer and more sure of herself, and when Marc glanced around he saw that she'd obviously decided he wasn't going to start frothing at the mouth and had walked across to join him. "That middle one—the one I'm using for an office—has no closets, and you can tell that the window was added much later." She pulled the bathroom door open for his inspection. "It's been enlarged and modernized, thank goodness. Five feet were taken off the middle bedroom to make room in here for the new tub."

The bathroom was light and airy, done in white and pale green, with plenty of mirrors to enlarge it even more. It, too, was full of plants, baskets of ferns and spider plants blending into the fern and bamboo wallpaper so well he couldn't tell where reality ended and fantasy started. "No tigers loose in there, are there?" He smiled teasingly at her as he drew back.

Paige laughed. "No, but Tyler calls it the 'Tarzan Room.' I guess I did get a little carried away with the plants."

"Looks nice." He stepped by her and strolled the other way, pausing to look into what was obviously Tyler's room, then stepping into the large room at the end. It was Paige's bedroom, and for the first time since he'd come into her home, Marc felt like the intruder he was. It was dim and scented with her perfume and that underlying woman smell of soap and bath powder and makeup that he found utterly irresistible. The bedspread was a muted swirl of mauves and blues, and the low dresser held only two cut-glass perfume bottles and what looked like a porcelain music box. He seemed to be surrounded by her, breathing her in through every pore, and suddenly he couldn't get enough of it. Unable to stop himself, he walked fully into the room, trailing his fingertips along the polished dresser top, the silk of it like living flesh, lightly touching the perfume bottle she must handle every day. He glanced into the mirror and saw her watching him uneasily from the doorway, arms clasped tightly across her chest, that worried little frown on her face again.

Their eyes met on glass, and for a taut, endless moment they stared at each other. She knows, Marc thought. She knows exactly what I'm thinking…how much I want her. And he did, he realized with a despairing wonder. It didn't matter that he'd just met her, that they'd traded no more than a few words. From the first instant their eyes had met, he'd been lost to whatever magic she wove. That's why he'd come up here—not because he wanted to see the house but because he wanted to see this room. *Her* room. He'd known the air would be heavy with the scent of her, and he'd wanted to lose himself in the essence of her, to touch the things she touched.

He took a deep breath and tore his gaze away. Keep this up, he told himself angrily, and you're going to wind up committed. He forced himself to stroll across to the deep bay window, his back to her. "They did a really good job on this, didn't they?" He rapped his knuckles against the inside glass and peered through it with feigned interest. The original window had been left intact with its myriad tiny leaded panes, the new one installed on the inside to preserve the integrity of the original design while weatherproofing the room.

"Yes. They...they did."

He stared at the window for a couple of moments as though he really gave a damn, then turned and walked back toward the door. "Nice house." She was still standing in the doorway, and she moved back as he neared, her gaze briefly brushing his, then sliding away as though not daring to meet his eyes. Which was probably just as well, Marc thought savagely as he stepped by her and strode toward the stairs. Heaven alone knew what she was likely to see there. He was making a fool of himself!

Tyler was crouched at the top of the stairs. He'd gathered up the damp towels and was patting the carpet cautiously with his hand. "I think it's dry, Mommy."

"Thank you, Tyler," Paige replied quietly. "How about putting those towels in the bathtub for me?"

"Okay." He bounced to his feet and headed for the bathroom.

His tattered yellow blanket lay where he'd left it, and Marc picked it up. "Getting a little old for this?"

Paige smiled. "He'll be back for it. Five minutes without it is his limit. I manage to sneak it into the laundry now and then when he's asleep, but if he wakes up before I'm done and finds it gone, there's heck to pay."

Marc laughed and tossed the faded blanket over the newel post where Tyler would see it. Then, knowing he should leave but not wanting to yet, he tipped his head back to look up at the offending skylight. "Does it leak often?"

"Often enough," Paige said disgustedly. "All the weather forecaster has to do is *predict* rain and it starts dripping."

Marc sensed more than heard her come up behind him, and although he knew it was impossible, he swore he could feel her body warmth against his bare back. A waft of musky perfume enveloped him, subtle yet so evocative it made his toes curl, and he had the sudden and completely insane urge to dispense with good manners and courtesy and all the other trappings of civilization and crush this woman's mouth under his in a kiss that would leave them both reeling.

It took all his willpower, but Marc kept his eyes on the skylight and his hands firmly in the hip pockets of his jeans. "I'm surprised it's lasted this long, to be honest about it." His voice sounded strained, and he breathed deeply, trying to relax the muscles in his stomach and chest. "It's a cheap skylight to start with—factory second, by the look of the flaws in it. And whoever installed it did a lousy job." She was standing beside him now, so close that when she tipped her head back her hair spilled across his arm. Marc flinched and clenched his teeth so tightly his jaw ached.

"What do you mean?" She frowned, looking at him.

"Flush," he said hoarsely. Her frown deepened and he dragged in another deep breath, forcing himself to tear his gaze from hers before something in his eyes or face gave him away and she had him arrested on the spot. "It's flush-mounted," he explained, trying to ignore the touch of her hair, the nearness of her. "It's set in a flat stretch of roof here, so it should be built up at least eighteen inches, not flush-mounted. During a heavy rain, water builds up around it, pushes up under the seal—and it leaks. You'd better have it replaced, and fast."

"Replaced?" The shock in her voice made Marc look down at her. She was staring up at the skylight, looking very pale and lost. "But I can't possibly—I mean, can't it be repaired somehow? Resealed?"

"Same thing will happen unless it's built up and sealed with metal flashing." For some reason Marc found himself hating to tell her this as he watched the hope in her eyes fade to despair. Yet there was no point lying to her. "Every time it rains, you're going to get water coming in, soaking the insulation, running along the joists. Eventually it'll rot the entire roof and ceiling, and you'll be looking at repair costs a hundred times greater than the cost of a new skylight.''

"But—'' She stopped, drawing in a deep breath. "Yes,'' she whispered despairingly. "Yes, I guess you're right.''

"You can always look on the bright side,'' he teased gently, suddenly finding it important to see her smile again. "It'll keep the bats and raccoons from moving in.''

It almost worked. A glimmer of a smile lifted Paige's mouth for a second, then vanished. Marc watched her walk slowly down the stairs, her shoulders slumped as though under the weight of the world. He felt his own shoulders droop in sympathy and caught himself, frowning. This wasn't his problem! Buying a century-old house was a gamble, and she should have known that before she sank what probably amounted to her life's savings into it. No one had forced her to buy in Toronto's downtown core, where most of the houses were like this one and the ones that weren't—the new town houses and condominiums—were priced out of sight. The real estate boom had brought every investor and fly-by-night renovator out of the woodwork, and the city core was filled with houses just like this, run down old places that had undergone cheap cosmetic surgery to hide their most obvious faults, then been resold at a profit.

Still frowning, growing more and more annoyed at himself for letting Paige MacKenzie's problems bother him, Marc followed her downstairs. He hadn't been under any delusions when he'd bought his half of Chestnut Manor: He'd *known* that it would cost a mint to restore the old house properly. So why, if his neighbor couldn't afford to do the same, had she bought the place at all? Why hadn't she just withdrawn her offer when his had come in, and let him buy the entire Manor as he'd wanted to in the first place? In spite of his annoyance, Marc had to smile at himself. He was acting like a spoiled kid who'd just had his favorite toy taken away.

Besides, he advised himself with a growing smile, he would much rather *watch* Paige MacKenzie than get angry with her. Because there was a good deal to watch. He found his eyes drawn to the silken flash of her legs as she strode in front of him across the living room, the swing of her hips under the well-fitted skirt. She was small-boned and slender, but what there was of her was superbly packaged. There wasn't a wasted angle or curve or indentation anywhere on her, and he swallowed a sigh of disappointment when they reached the kitchen and he had to take his eyes off her perfectly delectable little bottom and pretend to examine the kitchen cabinets with something even remotely nearing the same enthusiasm.

Four

Paige's eyes widened when she stepped into the kitchen. "Good grief! I didn't expect something so… complicated."

What she'd expected, Paige realized, were a couple of boards to replace the mop handle, a solution that would have worked well enough but would have rendered her kitchen all but useless. But Marc had anticipated that. He'd wedged three long pieces of cleanly planed lumber between the opposing sets of cupboards at ceiling height, positioned carefully so they wouldn't interfere with the doors on either side. Then he'd cut two shorter pieces and had set them upright like legs between the countertop and the bottom of the overhanging cupboard so the cupboard rested solidly on them. Supported at the bottom and braced firmly against the wall at the top, the cupboard now looked as though it would still be standing long after the rest of the house had crumbled into dust. And that wasn't all he'd done, she realized. All the broken glass had been cleaned up, and most of her remaining dishes were back in the cupboard.

"I don't know how to even begin thanking you." Paige turned to look at him, only to discover that her handyman neighbor hadn't been looking at the cupboards at all but at her. Those lake-blue eyes were still tracing the curve of her throat and cheek, and as they moved unhurriedly to meet her eyes, Paige was infuriated to feel the heat of a blush scald her cheeks. Darn it, why was she letting him affect her like this? She'd blushed more in the past day and a half than she had in the entire preceding twenty-seven years!

Without even wanting to, she found herself thinking about those few minutes upstairs with him. About that split second when their eyes had met in the mirror of her dressing table. That hungry look had sent a frisson of wanting through her so strong her breath had caught, and she'd had to call on every ounce of willpower to keep from turning and bolting. It hadn't been the blatant sexual attraction itself that had frightened her—she was old enough that a moment of mutual sexual awareness with a man, an awareness of herself and her own needs, didn't alarm her. It had been the aching emptiness, the yearning just to be held and caressed and comforted, that had nearly sent her running. That brief glimpse of her own weakness had terrified her.

Still, she found herself musing almost regretfully with a sidelong glance at her neighbor, it was too bad she'd never gotten the hang of casual affairs. She was well past the age of consent, and so was he. They'd probably be quite good for each other.

She had to swallow a sudden giggle, mildly shocked at the less-than-chaste direction her thoughts were taking. An hour ago she could have cheerfully murdered the man; now she was more or less contemplating seducing him. She dared to look at the subject of these uncharacteristic thoughts and found him gazing down at her, a faint frown marring his smooth, tanned forehead. His strong chin was smeared with grime where he'd absently run his dirty hand across it, and before she realized what she was doing, she found herself reaching up to wipe it off.

She could have sworn he flinched at her touch. "I don't bite, Mr. d'Angelo," she told him dryly. "Stand still for a minute and I'll wash that off." Stepping by him, she pulled a clean towel from the rack under the sink, then wet one corner of it and proceeded to wipe the dirt from his chin.

His mouth, which suddenly seemed distractingly close, curved in a beguiling smile. "Want to check my hands, too?"

Paige had to laugh. "Sorry. It's just habit. When I see a dirty face, I have this overwhelming urge to wash it. It comes from living with an active four-year-old."

"Then I'd say you definitely need an evening or two in the company of an adult," he murmured, his eyes examining her features with disturbing interest. They, too, seemed closer than they had been moments ago. "Starting with dinner tonight."

"Dinner?" She stared at him in surprise.

"Dinner." The smile widened, warm and deliciously inviting. "You remember dinner out, don't you? A man and a woman, a nice restaurant, candlelight, wine, dancing. It's a perfectly respectable evening pastime. People do it all the time."

"No," said Paige thoughtfully, concentrating on the smudge. "There's no one to look after Tyler, and—"

"I know a good baby-sitter."

"No." She said it more firmly this time, turning to put the towel aside. "I…can't."

"Can't?" He reached out and caught her wrist, turning her toward him. "Or won't?"

"In this instance," she teased lightly, "it amounts to the same thing, doesn't it?" She pulled her wrist free and turned toward the sink. "I can't, really. I have about thirty jars of barbecue sauce to make up and label tonight, a couple of hundred advertising flyers to fold, envelopes to address, stamps to lick. And I—" She stopped, looking into those azure eyes, which were unnervingly close to hers. And I don't need any involvements in my life right now, she nearly added. Not with a handsome, blue-eyed man who makes my heart do handstands every time he looks at me… But she didn't say it. Instead, she let her gaze slip aside. "I haven't got the time, Mr. d'Angelo. I'm sorry."

"So am I." He said it softly, his voice a husky purr of sound that made her breath catch slightly. "But don't think you're going to discourage me this easily, Paige."

He seemed to sway toward her, and Paige was utterly astounded to realize he was going to kiss her. Not only that, but she wasn't going to make even a token attempt to stop him. It was impossible, she told herself very calmly as she watched his eyes drop toward her. Absolutely and completely impossible...

"Mommy, is that cupboard gonna fall down again?"

Paige blinked. The blue eyes hanging above hers paused in their descent, then drew back swiftly, and Paige drew in an unsteady breath, feeling as though she'd just stepped off the edge of a cliff.

"Not a chance, short stuff," she heard a calm male voice say from somewhere above her. "But I want you to swear a solemn oath that you won't touch these uprights. They're jammed in there pretty tight, but if you bump one and knock it out, the whole thing could come down on top of you. Understand?"

"Yes," Tyler whispered, his eyes like saucers.

"Promise if you want something out of the cupboard you'll ask your mom?"

"Promise," Tyler repeated with feeling, eyeing the two supporting uprights with healthy respect. "I won't *touch* 'em!"

"That's good. Now, if I can get your mother to promise the same thing..."

Paige merely nodded, afraid to trust her voice.

"Good." Marc gave a quiet laugh. Then, to her intense relief, he stepped back and gestured toward the cupboard as though they'd never been discussing anything else. "You've got some serious problems here."

It took Paige a dizzied moment or two to realize that he was talking about her kitchen cabinet, and not about her refusal to go out with him. "I realize that. I plan to have all the cabinets replaced eventually, but in the meantime I'll hire someone to fix this one." Another unplanned expense, she added silently. Another drain on her already strained bank account.

"It's more serious than that. The plaster behind here is rotten." He tapped the wall with his knuckles, nodding toward the ceiling. "The bathroom's right above here, and it looks as though the plumbing's been leaking for years, rotting the wall. There's nothing to anchor the cabinet to."

Paige's heart sank. "Oh, no," she whispered. What else could possibly go wrong? "You mean I'll have to have the entire wall rebuilt?"

"That's one option. But if I were you, I'd tear it out completely. Having this little kitchen stuck right in the middle of the house, wedged between the living room and dining room, chops the house up too much. All that light coming in through the dining room walkout is wasted—none of it gets in here or the living room." He gestured toward the south-facing dining room, which even at this time of day was flooded with sunshine.

The table held a single place setting, and Paige gazed at the empty orange juice glass, cereal bowl and gnawed toast crusts with surprise. "Tyler, did you make your own breakfast?"

"Nope." Tyler was sitting on the floor in front of the open patio doors. A black squirrel was gazing hopefully at him, nose and forepaws pressed against the screen. "Marc made it for me."

"It was the easiest way of keeping him out from underfoot while I fixed the cabinet," Marc said with a smile. "Hope you don't mind."

But to Paige's intense surprise, she realized that she *did* mind! She knew she was being silly, that she should have been impressed by Marc's resourcefulness, his concern for Tyler's safety, but the thought of this interloper sharing a morning routine with her son that by rights was hers made her furious. She was overwhelmed by a flood of unfamiliar and confusing emotions: anger, jealousy, betrayal. And, under them all, fear. The fear that she was losing her son to this tall, blue-eyed stranger, who was prowling the confines of her kitchen as though he belonged here. Orange juice, she found herself thinking. She'd been trying to get Tyler to drink orange juice for months!

But Marc didn't seem to see the heat in her eyes. He gestured toward the dining room, where Tyler was now tossing out the leftover toast crusts to the squirrel. "Move the kitchen to the back. Knock that rear wall out about five feet or so to give you a nice breakfast nook overlooking the garden, and turn what's now kitchen into the dining room. Swing the staircase leading to the second floor around ninety degrees to act as a divider between it and the living room. Keep it open-concept, so you get the feel of division between the room without sacrificing light or airiness. Then—"

Paige gave a strangled laugh. "And just how am I paying for all of this architectural magic? I can't even afford the new kitchen cabinets yet. They were on *next* year's budget.''

Marc opened his mouth as though to say something, then shut it again on an impatient sigh and stared at the offending wall, hands on hips. ''Okay, let's take it one step at a time. My father owns Angel Construction. It's one of the best small construction companies in the business, and it specializes in renovations like this one. I'll have Pop take a look at this mess. If anyone can salvage it, he can. Maybe he can figure out how to put in enough solid bracing to hold the cabinetry in place until you decide what you want done. But you'll have to get that leak fixed first, and you may as well do it while the wall's torn out. I've got a battalion of plumbers coming tomorrow, and I'll send one over to take a look.''

Paige's eyes were getting wider and wider. ''But—''

Seeming not to even notice her interruption, Marc shrugged one bare shoulder toward the ceiling. ''I'll get Pop to see what he can do about that skylight, too. He can probably call in a favor or two and pick one up for you at below cost.''

''But—''

''And I noticed the plaster on the outside wall of that back bedroom you use as an office is rotten and pulling away. The only thing holding it together is the wallpaper. Either the roof's leaking and water's running down, or the mortar between the bricks on the outside wall has fallen out and the rain's just blowing in. Or it could be something as simple as a blocked downspout that can't carry the water away fast enough, forcing it up under the shingles. Either way, you could be looking at roof damage." He stared at the ceiling as though able to see right through it and the rooms above to the roof itself. "I'll have someone take a look. Then—"

"Hold it!" Paige threw both hands up, her voice loud enough to startle Marc into silence. He and Tyler stared at her. "I appreciate your concern, but I think you've overlooked one small fact—this is *my* house. All those things will be taken care of, but I'll take care of them myself. When I'm ready."

Marc frowned impatiently. "Then you'd better get ready in a big hurry, lady. Because every day that goes by increases the chances of serious structural damage."

"I'm quite aware of that." Actually she hadn't thought of it at all, but now that he'd mentioned it, Paige saw he was right. More costs. More worries. More sleepless nights trying to figure out how to—

"Look," Marc put in quietly. "Let's make a deal. I'll have the most critical problems taken care of for you, and you can pay me back when you've got the money."

"I don't take welfare." Paige said each word with quiet precision, feeling all the old, familiar angers starting to rise. She struggled to subdue them. "This house is my responsibility, and I'll take care of it myself."

"I'm not offering you welfare," Marc said quietly. "I'm offering you help."

"I don't need help!" She said it so loudly and fiercely that Marc blinked at her. "Yours or anyone else's. I appreciate your help with this cupboard, but everything's under control now.'' *My* control, she nearly added. ''Tell me how much I owe you for the lumber, and I'll pay you right now.''

He stared down at her, impatience etched across his face. ''You don't owe me anything for the lumber. It was just scrap.''

''I told you I don't accept charity, Mr. d'Angelo. This doesn't look like scrap lumber to me. How much?''

His eyes narrowed dangerously. ''You really are trying my patience, lady.''

''How much?''

''One jar of ginger jam.''

''I don't have any extra.''

''Then pay me later.''

''I don't like outstanding debts. How much?''

Marc's eyes narrowed even more. Then he gave a snort of laughter and turned away, shaking his head as he headed for the living room. ''Just call it an investment.''

''Investment?'' Paige stared after him suspiciously. ''For what?''

''For my future.'' He stopped in the middle of her living room and stood there, hands on hips, long legs spread wide, and slowly surveyed the room like a conquering warlord appraising hard-won territories. When they'd made full circuit of the room, his eyes met hers. He smiled tolerantly at her. ''Sooner or later you're going to realize that you're in over your head, and you're going to give up. When that happens, this half of the house will be mine, too. So you might say I have an interest in its well-being.''

"I have news for you, mister—the only well-being you'd better keep an eye on around here is your own. Because you'll be tottering around in a wheelchair before I give this house up!''

"Oh, don't be too sure of that.''

"Just how do you plan to get it away from me? Murder?''

"Nothing that dramatic.'' He grinned winningly at her. "If you don't give up and sell, I guess I'll just have to marry you.'' With that, he strolled toward the hole in her wall.

Paige stared at his retreating back, managing nothing more than a wordless sputter of fury. By the time she'd recovered enough to go after him, there was nothing left to shout at but one long leg that was rapidly disappearing through the hole. "Don't you dare come back in here!'' she shouted after him. "And stay out of my basement and off my roof and—''

"Mommy, why are you yelling at the wall?''

Paige's furious outburst faltered as she realized that she was doing precisely that. Marc had vanished, and Paige glowered at the hole as she struggled to get her temper under control. "This,'' she said to no one in particular, "is *impossible*.''

"What's impossible, Mommy?'' Tyler peered into the hole cautiously. "Is Marc coming back?''

"Not if he values his life.'' Paige gave the hole one last, angry look before turning away. "Tyler, I don't want you even talking to that man again.''

"But, Mommy—"

"Not one word," Paige said firmly. "Ever. Now help me get these jars of jam into the car so we can leave."

"But—" Tyler, seeing the expression her her face, subsided. "Okay," he muttered, giving the hole a longing glance before picking up a jar of jam and cradling it. "But I don't know why you were yelling at him. I think he's a nice man."

As she picked up the dish drainer and its precious cargo and started carrying it to the front door, Paige could have sworn she heard a quiet chuckle from the other side of the wall.

Marc found himself grinning as he made his way through the scattered tools and lumber littering his living room floor. He was in an ebullient mood for no particular reason, and he whistled as he strode into the kitchen. Beelzebub, stretched out in the sun in front of the big sliding doors leading out onto what would eventually be a brick patio, lifted his head. He got to his feet leisurely, stretched, yawned, then strolled over to rub against Marc's ankles.

"You're out of luck, you old reprobate. I'm just making coffee." Marc filled the kettle and plugged it in. Beelzebub did a slow shoulder roll and wound up on his back, big paws waving gently in the air. "Why don't you go out and hunt like a respectable cat, instead of hanging around in here, running my grocery bill up?" Bub began a roaring purr that said he knew perfectly well that Marc's complaint was nonsense.

A door slammed on the other side of the house. A

moment later a car door closed with an emphatic bang and Marc smiled in anticipation, reaching for the jar of instant coffee. Who was going to win this morning: Paige or the Volvo? The two of them had been having a battle of wills for the past week, although lately the old car seemed to be winning more often than it lost. There was silence for a moment, then the grinding whine of a car engine refusing to turn over. Marc's grin widened as he rooted through the clutter of tools, loose ceramic tiles and boxes of dry grout littering the countertop until he found a mug. He dumped out the finishing nails and sawdust, then rinsed it and tossed a generous scoop of coffee in. Round one to the Volvo.

The grinding continued as Paige tried the ignition again and again. Marc had a sudden image of her sitting behind the wheel, mouth compressed, eyes narrowed with anger as she set her will against the car's. He had just about decided that the car was going to win the entire bout when the engine started with a roar. Then it sputtered and died.

"Needs a new battery," he told the cat. "And a tune-up."

The kettle started to whistle. Marc made his coffee and carried the mug over to the tool-covered table, clearing a space with his elbow as he sat down. He found himself craving a cigarette suddenly. Fighting down the urge, he took a cautious sip of the coffee instead, running a critical eye over the floor-to-ceiling glass doors leading to the backyard. Last night it had been nothing but a big hole covered with plastic sheeting, and he shook his head wonderingly at the speed with which his father had installed the doors. The unpainted frame fitted the opening perfectly, and Marc knew that the doors would glide open and closed effortlessly. There was simply no room in Vincenzo d'Angelo's life for anything less than perfection.

Outside, the car engine turned over and caught, and this time Paige managed to keep it running. "She's something else, isn't she?" he asked Bub. The cat strolled toward him, stepping daintily around the piles of lumber and tools cluttering the bare plywood subflooring. "Got a mind of her own, though. And a stubborn streak a block wide."

He found himself smiling again as a surge of adolescent happiness sailed through him. Bub jumped lightly onto his lap and made himself comfortable, and Marc started stroking the cat's thick fur, thinking absently of the feel of Paige's skin. She was stubborn and hardheaded, maybe, he found himself musing. But there was something about her that made him feel like a kid again.

He hadn't felt this way since…when? His smile broadened with the remembering. Ninth grade. He recalled a mane of golden hair, big blue eyes, a mouth that tasted like berries and cream. The memories came back in a rush, so erotically vivid that his body, even twenty-four years and a good number of other memories later, responded with a vital energy that startled him. Skin so soft to his inexperienced touch that he'd been half afraid to touch her for fear of hurting, too desperate for the wanting not to.

Marc chuckled again. Those first clumsy caresses

had been astonishingly innocent, yet the experience had provided him with enough erotic fantasies to get him through high school and right into college, where the embraces had become much more frequent and much less innocent. But of all the women and all the embraces in those intervening years, none had ever held the magic and wonder of those first few stolen minutes. Until now.

Marc gave a snort of wry laughter that made Bub flick his ears. Don't get carried away, my friend, he warned himself. If those twenty years have taught you anything, it should be that love's as elusive as a unicorn. You don't knock down a brick wall one morning and find your life changed.

He winced. That damned wall! He should get started on it right away. But for the life of him he couldn't generate even the slightest enthusiasm, in spite of the fact he wasn't going to be able to finish the living room until he had. But in some odd way the hole had become more important than the wall it was in. It was like one of those magical doorways in a kid's fairy tale, he thought idly, leading to an enchanted land where dreams come true. Enchanted lands where one might even find a unicorn...

He gave his head an impatient shake. It's just a hole in the wall. No magic doorway, no enchanted lands, no unicorns. Just a hole. And a link, however tenuous, to a woman who fascinated him greatly.

To her surprise, Paige found herself humming as she paid the cabdriver and started up the walk to her front door. It didn't seem possible after all she'd been through today with that miserable car, but she felt absolutely ebullient. Even seeing her mother's big gray Mercedes parked at the curb didn't give her the little jab of guilt it normally would have.

She had her keys half out of her bag before she realized that the double doors to the house were open. Not only that, but the inner doors to both Marc's side of the house and hers were ajar. Frowning, she stepped into her living room. Voices came wafting from the kitchen: unfamiliar male voices. The back of Paige's neck prickled and she stood there for a moment, poised between calling the police and facing the intruders herself.

But in the next instant the decision was made for her. There was a squeal of child's laughter and Tyler came flying out of the kitchen with a long-legged young giant of a man in hot pursuit. He caught Tyler and swept him up into the air and Tyler screamed with delight.

They both saw her at the same instant. The young man, clad only in tight blue jeans and a construction worker's tan, draped Tyler unceremoniously over one broad shoulder and grinned cheerfully at her. "Hi!"

"Hi, Mommy!" Tyler shouted, seemingly delighted to be hanging upside down over a complete stranger's shoulder. He peered around his captor's tanned rib cage and waved at her. "Look at me! I'm a acrobat!"

"Who—?" But Paige's astonished query went unanswered. The man turned and strode back into the kitchen without even a backward glance, her son draped over his shoulder like the spoils of war.

Paige was still standing there, stunned, when a flash of movement at the top of the stairs made her look up. The young man hanging over the upstairs railing and grinning down at her could have been a twin to the one who had kidnapped Tyler. It took her a moment to realize it was Greg d'Angelo. "Hey, sweetheart," he said in a passable Bogart lisp, "they're getting ready to take it out. Give Vic a shout and tell him Marc wants him on the roof."

"Taking it out?" Paige echoed faintly.

"The skylight." Still grinning, he vaulted lightly over the railing and landed halfway down the stairs, then galloped the rest of the way down and headed for the kitchen. "Your pop's on the roof with Gabriel, if you wanna talk to him."

"Daddy's *where*?" To herself, Paige added almost despairingly, "With *who*?" She had a sudden image of her father perched on the roof with a silver-winged angel, both of them in three-piece suits, leather briefcases in hand, discussing the latest developments in the financial world.

She'd walked into a nightmare, she decided dizzily. Her father could not be on the roof, with or without a watchful angel. Harrington J. Pricefield liked both feet planted firmly on the ground, where he could rule his part of that financial world with the meticulous attention to detail that had made him one of the most respected financial consultants in the country.

A burst of husky male laughter broke her reverie. Paige's eyes narrowed and she took a deep breath. She was going to get to the bottom of this if it was the last thing she ever did, she decided as she started toward the kitchen. And while she was at it, she was going to rescue her son from the brawny young Viking who had abducted him. And then she was going to get her hands on the one man she suspected was behind all this—Marc d'Angelo.

But a moment later Paige realized two things: Her house had been taken over by a tribe of husky, blue-eyed giants, and her son wasn't remotely interested in being rescued.

The kitchen and dining room seemed to be full of men, all of them well-muscled and deeply tanned, and it took her a moment to realize that there were really only four. One of them was Vincenzo d'Angelo, dressed in jeans and a bright red work shirt. He and a younger man were sitting at her dining table, engrossed in what looked like blueprints. Tyler was sitting contentedly in the older man's lap, playing with the level Marc had given him. The other two—Greg and the one who had kidnapped Tyler—were in her tiny kitchen, tearing the wall apart.

The set of cabinets that had fallen were stacked along one wall of the dining room. Mute with astonishment, Paige watched as the two men tore away chunks of the wall, the rotten plasterboard crumbling like cheese in their hands.

"What are you doing?" she finally managed to whisper.

"Hi. I was wondering when you'd show up." Marc placed his hand comfortably on her waist and squeezed by her. "Your mother said you'd had to leave your car at the supply place up on Finch Avenue and take a cab home. I sent T.K. up to have a look at it.''

''T.K?'' Paige echoed faintly.

Marc smiled. ''Georgio Bianchi, better known as T.K., as in 'The Kid.' He's only sixteen, but he knows more about cars than Henry Ford himself. If anyone can get that old heap of yours running, he can.'' Then, as though just seeing her confusion, he gave a quiet laugh. ''Sorry, forgot you don't know everyone here. That's my oldest brother, Roman, at the table with Pop.'' He gestured at the other two. ''Greg you've met. The other one's another brother, Vic.''

Vic grinned at her, then looked over her head at Marc. ''You still need us both up there, or can we finish this?''

''Gabe's got it under control for the moment. Finish what you're doing, then get this mess cleaned up so Paige can use the kitchen.'' Marc looked down at her, his hand still draped over the swell of her upper hip. ''It's going to take us a few days to get things back to normal, but we'll try to keep the uproar to a minimum.''

''What are you doing in here?'' Paige asked despairingly. ''Where's my mother, what's my father doing on the roof, and what are you doing to my skylight?''

Marc blinked at her as though unable to fathom why she might be upset. ''Your mother's still up in my second-floor bathroom, I think—she wanted to have a look at the tub. And your dad's watching Gabriel replace the skylight.''

''Replace…?'' Paige closed her eyes and rubbed

the spot between her brows where a dull ache was threatening to settle. She took a deep breath. "Who," she asked very calmly, "is Gabriel? And why is he replacing my skylight?"

"Gabriel's one of my brothers, and we're replacing your skylight because it leaks, remember?" He smiled, looking quite pleased with himself. "By sheer chance, Pop's doing a reno in Riverdale that includes replacing a couple of small skylights with one big one. The two they took out are in perfect shape—Pop had them sitting in the back of the pickup when I called him this morning. Won't cost you a thing."

"I told you I didn't want your charity!" Paige felt like crying with sheer frustration. Why wouldn't *anyone* listen to her! She wrenched away from Marc's hand and strode into the living room, then stopped short with a gasp of horror. "My God!" she whispered, eyes widening. "What is *that*?"

Five

That was the biggest cat Paige had ever seen in her life. It was sitting dead center in the bay of her front window, staring out across the street, looking like the stone effigy of some ancient Egyptian god. At her voice, the cat turned its massive orange head slowly and fixed her with a blazing copper stare. Then it gave a slow, derisive blink and turned back to the window.

"That's Bub. Beelzebub," Marc said conversationally.

"Get it out of here." Paige enunciated each word with precision. "If I see that animal even looking at Tyler, I'll turn it into a rug."

Neither Marc nor his cat seemed to take the threat very seriously. "He's harmless."

"Nothing that big can possibly be harmless. And apart from the fact that I don't want my house or my preserves covered with fur, I don't like cats, Mr. d'Angelo. And look what it's done to my rug!'' She glared at the Oriental rug, or more precisely, at its royal-blue border. Up the very middle of that border, as tidy as a row of stitched embroidery, ran a line of large, dusty footprints. Cat footprints.

"You know what they say about people who don't like cats," Marc gibed her gently. "Usually people who don't like cats are people who like to be in charge all the time. They don't like having anything around that won't listen to them."

"That certainly shouldn't apply to me," Paige shot back dryly. "I can't remember the last time anyone listened to anything I said. For instance," she added, giving him a frosty glare, "I could have sworn I told you to keep your hands off my skylight. Or maybe I just imagined the whole thing."

"Oh, for crying out loud." Marc swept his fingers through his hair, leaving it in tumbling disarray. "Your father said to remind you it's an investment."

"In *your* house?"

"In *your* house, damn it. Not only is it going to keep you dry, but it's increasing the resale value."

Trust her father to see only the dollars-and-cents practicality of it, Paige thought angrily. "Leave the old one in and get off my roof."

Marc's eyes held hers with what she could have sworn was deliberate challenge. "It's too late. The old one's out by now."

"Then put it back in."

"Can't." His smile held a touch of triumphant finality. "It cracked when we pried it out. Thing's sitting in about three pieces now."

Paige had a raging desire to slap that self-satisfied smile off his face, but she managed to hang on to her temper. "Then take it out and cover the hole with plastic! I'll order a new one and have it installed myself."

"Gabriel's already sealing it." Then, as though wearying of the game, Marc stared down at her impatiently. "Quit being a pain in the neck, Paige. It's done. And maybe one day you'll even thank me for tracking down a free skylight and installing it for nothing."

"Oh, I'm going to—" Just what she was going to do, Paige didn't quite know, and she had her hand up and poised before she realized that slapping him soundly was going to accomplish nothing.

Marc's gaze held hers steadily. "If smacking me in the mouth will make you feel better, go ahead. But that skylight stays."

There was a matter-of-fact finality to his voice that raised Paige's hackles, but before she could respond, Tyler padded into the room, his blanket and ever-present level tucked under his arm. "Mommy, why are they knockin' down the wall?"

"Ask your friend. He seems to be in charge of things around here."

"We're just tearing out the bad parts, short stuff." Marc playfully tweaked Tyler's snub nose between his fingers. "We're going to put in some solid cross beams, then replaster the wall and put the cabinets back up. Unless," he added with a pointed look at

Paige, "your mother stops being so hostile and pig-headed and takes my advice about tearing it down altogether."

"Have you ever thought of joining the Russian army? Just think—that way you could march in and tell entire nations how to run their lives."

"And have you ever thought that maybe you're carrying this independence thing a little too far?" His eyes bit into hers. "You've made your point. Now maybe it's time you backed off and admitted you could use some help."

"I don't need—"

"Oh, wow, Mommy! Lookit the cat!"

"Tyler!" Paige lunged for him, too late. He slipped through her fingers like an eel and raced toward Bub, but before she could take a step after him, Marc caught her arm.

"He's all right," he said calmly. "Old Bub's raised half a generation of d'Angelo kids and is working on his second, between grandchildren and cousins. He loves kids."

"It'll eat him alive!" Paige held her breath as Tyler dropped the level and blanket and landed on his knees beside the huge cat. It turned to look at him curiously, its head nearly level with his. Then it stretched out and touched its nose to Tyler's in a gesture that sent Tyler into gales of delighted giggles.

"It kissed me, Mommy!"

"Tyler, no! Oh…give me strength!" This last was to herself as Tyler bounced to his feet and wrapped both arms around the cat's midsection. He lifted it and started walking back toward her, small face

frowning with the effort. Bub seemed quite unconcerned about it all, hanging limply in Tyler's arms,
his huge head under Tyler's chin, back paws and tail
dragging on the floor. His broad feline face looked
utterly blissful, and Paige started to relax slightly.
"Don't step on his tail, honey. And don't drag him
around too long. He's an old cat and deserves at least
a bit of respect."

If Marc noticed that the cat had gone from "it" to
"he," he didn't let on. He just smiled and walked
back into the kitchen, Tyler padding earnestly along
behind him.

"Paige? Paige dear, is that you? Oh. There you
are." To Paige's astonishment, her mother's head
popped out of the hole in the wall. She smiled and
stepped into Paige's living room. Straightening, she
started brushing plaster and brick dust off her navy
and white designer suit. "My, that's awkward to get
through. You ought to make it bigger, don't you
think?"

"Bigger?" Paige stared at her mother, then shook
her head disbelievingly. "Mom, what *are* you doing?"

"Looking at Marc's bathroom. Have you seen it
yet? It's lovely—I must show it to your father. He's
been talking about having a whirlpool tub installed,
and—"

"Mother!" Paige didn't know if she was upset
more over her mother's easy use of Marc's first name
or the fact she didn't seem particularly disturbed at
finding her daughter's living room half demolished.
"How could you just...I mean, you've never been

interested in bathrooms before! And you can't just go wandering through someone's house looking at—''

"Of course I've been interested in bathrooms," her mother put in. "Everyone's interested in bathrooms. And I hardly just walked in uninvited. Marc gave me a delightful tour. He really is the nicest young man. Why haven't I heard about him before?''

"I—'' Paige stopped, then sighed heavily. "Oh, to hell with it.'' She smiled and kissed her mother's cheek. "Thanks for bringing Tyler home. I'm sorry I'm late. There was an accident on the parkway, and traffic was backed up for miles.''

"Heavens, don't worry about it.'' Her mother dismissed the matter with a wave of her hand. "I have a key, remember. Although we hardly need it, with that lovely Marc to let us in. We've been having the most marvelous time.'' Then she looked worriedly at Paige. "Really, darling, thinking of you driving that dreadful old car gives me nightmares. It's going to leave you stranded out in the wilds one day, and you'll be murdered or something.''

In spite of herself, Paige had to smile. Her mother's idea of the "wilds'' was any part of Toronto that wasn't Rosedale, that sedate, old-monied enclave where the Pricefields had lived for three generations.

"I wish you'd let me give you the BMW. I don't use it, you know. If I need a car during the day I use the Mercedes, and when we go out in the evening, your father insists on using the Jaguar. Or for that matter, your birthday's coming up—''

"No.'' Paige held up both hands. "No BMWs, no surprise birthday cars. Mom, I love you dearly for worrying about me, but I can manage. On my own. The Volvo just needs a tune-up."

Her mother gave a sniff, obviously not believing a word of Paige's protest but familiar enough with the old argument to know there was no point in continuing. "All right," she conceded. "I won't mention it again. That outfit looks very nice, by the way. You always could wear that color well."

"Brown goes well with her mood," put in a husky male baritone. Marc strolled in, not bothering to look at her. "What did you think of the bathroom, Mrs. Pricefield? Is that the kind of whirlpool you're interested in?"

"It's marvelous," Paige's mother gushed. "And for heaven's sake, call me Maggie—all my friends do."

Paige stared at her mother, scarcely believing what she'd just heard. *Maggie?* This was the woman who'd been known to freeze new acquaintances with a single chilling glance for daring to call her "Margaret" too soon.

"I'll have Harrington give you a call about it next week."

"That'll be fine." Marc gave Paige's mother a dazzling smile, then nodded toward the hole. "If you'll excuse me, I want to check on the skylight."

"Of course." Paige's mother peered after him as Marc slipped through the hole into his side of the house. "Would you remind my husband that we're meeting the Blacks for dinner at the club tonight, Marc? It's getting late."

"You mean you *knew* Daddy was on the roof?" Paige demanded in astonishment.

"Of course." Her mother looked at Paige oddly. "Dear, what *is* the matter with you today? You seem a little…befuddled."

"I can't imagine why," Paige replied serenely. "First my kitchen cabinet tries to kill me, then my car breaks down, then I come home to find my house taken over by people I've never seen before, my father on the roof, my mother clambering around a half-finished house, looking at a strange man's bathroom, my skylight torn out—and the day's not over yet."

"I don't know why you sound so upset." Her mother looked mildly affronted. "Marc seems to have everything under control."

"That's just the problem! He's come in and taken over my entire life. I can't turn around without falling over him. Would you believe he even answers my phone?"

Her mother smiled fondly. "Isn't it marvelous that you've got someone around to give you a hand when you're so busy, dear? And it's *so* nice to be on good terms with one's neighbors. He seems quite taken with you, you know."

Paige opened her mouth to protest, then subsided with a resigned sigh. It was no use. However Marc had won her family over, he'd done it well. Her mother was convinced he was the greatest thing in good-neighbor relations since backyard barbecues, and her father was probably contemplating putting him in the family business by now.

"What, dear?"

"Nothing, Mother. I just— Daddy!" Paige, who had decided that nothing else could possibly surprise her that afternoon, gaped at her father as he stepped through the hole in front of her. If she'd seen him in the street, she wouldn't have recognized him, jacket discarded, shirt streaked with dirt and sweat. To add insult to injury, he'd rolled his sleeves up carelessly and had loosened the knot in his tie. "What in heaven's name have you been doing?" she asked in astonishment.

He broke into a delighted smile and embraced her warmly. "Paige! How are you doing, honey?"

"*I'm* all right. But I'd like to know what you think you're doing scrambling around on my roof."

"Just making sure my little girl's going to be dry in her bed tonight," he teased her, kissing her on the forehead. Marc stepped through the hole just then, and her father turned to him, holding out his hand. "Well, son, thanks for the tour. I'm impressed."

She'd heard everything now, Paige decided. She couldn't remember ever having heard her father call anyone "son" before, yet here he was greeting Marc as though he were a beloved member of the family.

He turned back to her then, frowning as he looked closely at her. "You look tired, princess. You need a vacation. I'm flying to Amsterdam tomorrow. Why don't you come with me? Tyler won't mind spending a few days with his grandmother."

Paige smiled wearily. "Dad, we've been through all this. Right now I'm one jump ahead of my orders; if I take even one day off, I'll never get caught up."

"You're wearing yourself out, princess. And you

have to think of Tyler. He never sees you anymore. What's it going to do to him if you make yourself sick over a silly pot of jam?''

"Dad..." Paige stopped, struggling to catch her anger. As it always did, her father's apparent inability to understand both saddened and annoyed her. Saddened her because she hated to see him trying so desperately to help her, only to have the daughter he adored spurn every offer of assistance, every word of advice. Annoyed her because she couldn't get him to realize that she was an adult now, responsible for her own problems. He just couldn't seem to see that she was too old to let Harrington J. Pricefield "take care" of things. She realized her father was looking at her expectantly, and she forced herself to smile. "Dad, Tyler's not a baby anymore. And I'm Harrington J. Pricefield's daughter, remember? I'm not going to do anything stupid.''

"Precisely my point," her father grumbled. "You *are* Harrington J. Pricefield's daughter, and you don't have to be doing this. There's plenty of room for you and Tyler at home. And if you insist on working, I can find you something down at the firm with sensible hours and twice the money you'll ever make with this jam thing.''

Knowing the man couldn't possibly be serious, yet surprised at the easy way he made a joke of his daughter's business, Marc gave Paige's father a sharp look. But he was even more surprised when he realized by the expression on Harrington J. Pricefield's face that he hadn't been joking at all.

What the hell was the matter with the man? Marc

asked himself angrily. Had the last umpteen years of wheeling and dealing with his fellow financiers down in the concrete canyons of Bay Street turned his heart to stone? He glanced at Paige, and the desolate hurt in her eyes made his own heart sink.

"What did you think of the skylight?" he interjected smoothly, stepping between Paige and her father. His eyes brushed Paige's as he turned toward the older man.

"Fits the bill exactly! That brother of yours does fine work. Have him drop by the house next week, and we'll discuss what I want done with the sun room."

"And you must look at the whirlpool bathtub, dear," his wife put in promptly. "It's exactly what we're looking for."

Marc glanced at Paige over her mother's shoulder. She was looking at him, her eyes warm with tentative gratitude as she realized that he had deliberately distracted her father from what was by now a well-rehearsed lecture. He offered her a conspiratorial smile and was inordinately pleased to see the corner of her mouth tilt upward in response, and he suddenly felt like a kid sharing a secret.

But the respite he'd given Paige didn't last. Her father looked down at her again. "Have you thought my offer over, sweetheart? About selling the GingerBread Preserves name to that company in Montreal, I mean. They'll pay you well, and they can reach markets you haven't even heard of. Then you can give up this house—rent it or get Marc to renovate it and sell it for a handsome profit." He smiled

down at her. "What do you say, princess? Do I call
Dupris on Monday and tell him—"

"Tell him no," Paige said firmly. "I'm not giving
GingerBread up, Dad. And I'm not giving this house
up." Marc had his mouth open to try another tactic
at distracting her father when she suddenly smiled,
her eyes sparkling with delight. "Besides," she added
breathlessly, obviously hardly able to contain her excitement, "Cabbages and Kings wants my jam."

He frowned and gestured impatiently. "Strictly
small-time, Paige. They'll nickel-and-dime you to
death."

Marc could have sworn Paige flinched. She looked
down swiftly, but not before he'd seen the childlike
excitement in her eyes vanish like a snuffed candle
flame. And in that split second, he could have quite
cheerfully slugged Pricefield on his obstinate jaw.

"Cabbages and Kings is one of the best restaurants
in the area," Paige said softly.

"Yuppies," her father replied derisively. "If you
want to go after restaurant trade, do it properly. Go
down to Winston's or the Royal York or—"

"Actually, Cabbages and Kings is probably the
perfect place to start," Marc interjected. Paige's father looked at him sharply. He obviously wasn't used
to having his opinions challenged, and his face darkened with annoyance. Marc held his stare evenly. "I
know Sean and DiCarlo. They'd rather do without
than settle for second best. They're also recognized
as *the* trendsetters in Toronto's restaurant trade. If
they carry your daughter's product, every restaurateur
in the city will know about it within hours. And there

won't be one of them who'll want to be left off the bandwagon. She couldn't ask for a better endorsement.''

Pricefield gave a skeptical grunt. ''We'll see.'' He looked down at Paige, dropping his arm around her shoulders. ''Think about that Montreal offer, princess. And in the meantime, do you need anything? New clothes? Money?''

''No, Dad,'' Paige whispered. ''I'm all right.''

Watching the two of them, Marc felt anger rise like bile in his throat. Couldn't the man see she was an adult? he found himself thinking heatedly. Couldn't he see past the little girl she'd once been to the strong, capable woman and mother she was? Stand back and let her grow up! he felt like shouting. He suddenly realized that Pricefield was looking at him.

''Keep an eye on my little girl here, will you?'' He hugged Paige against him, smiling down at her. ''I worry about her living down here all alone. I don't mind telling you that knowing you're next door has taken a load off my mind.''

''I'd be absolutely delighted to keep an eye on your daughter,'' Marc replied softly, looking straight at Paige.

To her horror, Paige felt herself blush furiously. ''I can take care of myself, Daddy,'' she said decisively, giving Marc a killing look. ''And Mr. d'Angelo hasn't time to watch over me. He's going to be much too busy repairing my plumbing, my skylight and my living-room wall. Aren't you, Mr. d'Angelo?''

But Marc just shrugged carelessly, his grin widening. ''My brothers can handle all that without any trouble. After all, this summer *is* supposed to be kind of a vacation for me, and if your father wants me to—''

"He doesn't,'' Paige assured him sweetly, linking arms with her parents and starting to lead them gently toward the door. "I'm glad you could drop by, Daddy. And thanks again for watching Tyler for me, Mom.''

It was nearly nine that evening by the time Paige got Tyler bathed and into bed and her life back to some recognizable order. Alone at last, relishing the solitude, she treated herself to an all-too-rare soak in a tub brimming with hot water and scented oils, and by the time she'd changed into jeans and a big T-shirt, she felt more relaxed than she had in weeks.

She smiled as she padded down to the kitchen, piling her steam-damp hair into a loose knot and securing it with a handful of pins as she went. You're on your way, Ms. MacKenzie, she congratulated herself. Cabbages and Kings thinks your ginger jam is the best thing in nouvelle cuisine since sushi, and Cheese-It Deli can't get enough of your chili sauce and barbecue spice! She skipped down the last two stairs with a quiet laugh, wishing she had someone to celebrate with. That was the one unsatisfying part of being alone—brimming over with happiness like this and having no one to share it with. Tyler was too young, the few friends she'd stayed in touch with after Peter's death couldn't fathom what she was doing, let alone understand *why* she was doing it, and her parents…well, they were still waiting for her to grow tired of it all and move back home with Tyler.

Thinking of her parents, of the impatience on her father's face when she'd told him about Cabbages and Kings this afternoon, took the edge off her good mood. She jammed her hands into the pockets of her jeans and wandered into the kitchen, feeling restless and hungry. She opened the fridge, stood staring at the sparse contents for a moment or two, then poured herself a glass of orange juice. Nothing else caught her interest and she closed the door with a sigh, gazing around her kitchen. Vic and Greg had left the place surprisingly tidy, the big sheet of plastic they used to protect the sink folded to one side, the counters washed, her food processor and canisters back in place. What had been the wall between the kitchen and dining room was nothing but an open network of studs and cross beams, and Paige was mildly annoyed to realize that Marc had been right about how much bigger the house looked with that wall gone. Maybe he was right about all of it, she brooded. Maybe she should think about knocking the wall out and—

She shook her head impatiently. Forget it. You can't afford a tenth of the renovation he was talking about.

Still restless, she opened a cupboard and surveyed the contents. She pulled out the box of chocolate chip cookies and helped herself to one, eyeing the big blue enamel stockpot sitting by the sink. You should get started on that spaghetti sauce, she told herself. Two dozen jars of it. The Church Street Gourmet Shoppe had wanted them yesterday, but there'd been the ginger jam to make for Cabbages and Kings, then the dozen or so little gift baskets of sample jams and spices for the Lady Jane Boutique. She sighed and bit into another cookie. If she could just get ahead on her orders! She always seemed to be one leap ahead of catastrophe, madly scrambling around every night, trying to fill this small order or that, never able to make up an excess of any one product. Time was a problem, but the biggest problem was money. She had to sell one small order to finance the next and never had enough in the bank to build up an inventory of either supplies or product.

There had to be a better way!

Still munching on the cookie, Paige wandered into the small dining room and stared out the big glass doors into the night. Her reflection gazed back at her and she smiled humorlessly, lifting her glass in a toast. "Here's looking at you, kid," she said aloud. "Congratulations on your big breakthrough."

"If you'd waited five more minutes," said a husky male voice from behind her, "we could have done that properly."

Paige started so badly she nearly spilled the juice. Wide-eyed, she stared at the reflection that had appeared beside hers in the darkened window.

Marc smiled. "I didn't know if you had any unbroken wineglasses left or not, so I brought a couple over."

"You...what?"

"Glasses." His smile widened, and he held up his left hand so she could see the bottle of wine and two long-stemmed glasses.

She gaped at the reflected bottle, then at him. Then, slowly, she turned around.

"And if you'll find a vase for *these*," he added, bringing his other hand from behind him with a flourish, "I'll pour us both a glass of wine so we can finish that toast."

These, to Paige's astonishment, were flowers. Dozens of flowers, rainbow-hued and fragrant. Their perfume filled the air and she reached for them wonderingly. "But…but what are they for?"

"You." He gazed down at her, his rain-blue eyes filled with warmth. "You done good, Paige MacKenzie. Cabbages and Kings is a tough market to crack. You deserve to be congratulated properly."

"But—" She gazed up at him in confusion.

"No buts, Paige," he said quietly, his eyes holding hers. "You did something to be proud of today."

Paige felt a delicate blush warm her cheeks. She let her gaze slide away from his, smiling as she sniffed the flowers. "They're beautiful. Thank you."

"Anytime. Now that I know it just takes flowers to make you smile, I'll bring you gardensful."

"You went to a lot of trouble," she said shyly. "All the stores around here are closed."

"You're worth it," Marc told her carelessly. "And celebrating alone isn't much fun."

Paige looked up, startled. Then she gave a quiet laugh. "I have to admit I'd never have expected this from you. The way you've been running roughshod through my life, I didn't take you for the sentimental type."

"And what type did you take me for?"

"Oh, the hard-nosed, pragmatic type. Like my father. Dedicated to getting the job done, regardless of the cost."

Marc nearly laughed, silently thanking whatever whim had made him go out and chase down those flowers. There had been a moment, just as he'd slipped through the hole into Paige's living room, that he'd cursed himself for a sentimental fool and had nearly called the whole thing off. The only thing that had stopped him was the memory of the disappointment in Paige's eyes when her father had dismissed her triumph with Cabbages and Kings. For some reason it had made him think of a few disappointments of his own, the hurt of having dreams dashed. Now, as he drank in the tentative delight on her face, he was glad he'd yielded to that silly whim.

"I used to be. Until I realized that goals are sometimes less important than the getting there." He held up the wine. "Got a corkscrew?"

"Top drawer, on the left." Paige was looking up at him curiously. "What changed your mind?"

Marc shrugged, rummaging through the drawer. He found the corkscrew and started to open the wine. "When I was a kid, my dream was to own a construction company. But I didn't want a small family affair like Pop had. I wanted to go into the big time—megaprojects, megabucks. I used to hang around the big building sites downtown and fantasize what it would be like to be straw boss of something that big, to watch those huge office towers grow up out of nothing like magic mushrooms, the sky full of cranes, a hundred hard hats on a shift."

Paige pulled a vase out of a lower cupboard and started filling it with water, but her attention was clearly on Marc. "And?" she urged. "Did the little boy get his dream?"

Marc smiled. "In spades. It took about fifteen years, but finally I didn't have to sneak onto building sites anymore or hang over plywood hoardings to watch what was going on." He paused, staring at the wine.

"But the reality didn't live up to the dream," Paige said, putting the flowers into the water and fussing with them for a minute.

Marc watched her thoughtfully. "Exactly. I got into construction because I loved watching a project go from nothing but an empty lot and a pile of raw material to a completed building. Translating those two-dimensional lines on a blueprint into a three-dimensional reality was the perfect alchemy to me. It was like taking a stack of musical scores and a hundred-piece orchestra and winding up with Beethoven's Fifth. Pure magic!" He realized that Paige was staring up at him in fascination. He laughed and pulled the cork out of the bottle. "The reality, of course, is that success is often its own punishment. The more successful we got, the busier I got, until I was spending fifteen hours a day in the office. One day I realized I hadn't set foot on a site in over six months."

"And you decided to get out of it?"

Marc's smile was humorless. "Not then. When you work as hard as I had for a dream, you don't give it up that easily." He started pouring wine into the glasses, his smile fading. "No, it took another year. One day I got a call that Ken, my partner, had died of a heart attack while inspecting one of our projects. Three weeks later one of my best friends had a coronary in the middle of a business meeting." He looked at Paige.

"There's something about burying two of your best friends within three weeks of each other that makes you think about your own mortality. I came home from Mike's funeral and took a long, hard look in the mirror. What I saw scared the hell out of me. I was fifteen pounds overweight, smoked and drank too much and had forgotten the meaning of the word *relax*." He gave a snort of rueful laughter. "Five days later, I'd sold my company, thrown my cigarettes out and began working out at the local gym. But I decided that if I wanted to make any real changes in my life, I had to get back in touch with the things that used to be important. So I bought this house and decided to take the summer off to fix it up."

"And then?"

"Pop wants Gabriel and me to take over Angel Construction so he can retire."

"Is that what you want?"

She asked it as though it were the most normal question in the world. And yet in that instant, Marc realized it was the one thing he'd never asked himself. He'd spent the last few weeks asking every question *but* that one, trying to solve the problem with an engineer's logic when all he'd had to do was listen to his own feelings. "Yes." He gazed down at her in surprise. The answer was so obvious. Why hadn't he figured it out on his own? "Yeah, I think it is. I'd forgotten how much I enjoy working with my hands, watching a project go together like a jigsaw puzzle, sweating the small stuff. I feel like I've come home."

"Then go for it." Paige gave the flowers a final pat, then smiled up at him. "Trust your feelings, Marc. They won't let you down."

"I'm beginning to do just that," Marc murmured, handing her one of the glasses. He wasn't thinking about his feelings for Angel Construction, and by the way she quivered when his fingers brushed hers, he was certain she wasn't either. He touched his glass to hers, feeling himself being drawn into those autumn-hued eyes. "To GingerBread Preserves, Paige."

"And to Angel Construction," she whispered. "May your new life be a happy and successful one."

Marc took a swallow of the wine, yet he hardly tasted it. He found himself mesmerized by Paige, watching avidly as she sipped the wine, his eyes drawn helplessly to her mouth. Her lips were half parted and moist, and he felt the blood pound in his temples as she drew the tip of her tongue across the full bow of her upper lip to capture a stray drop of Burgundy.

Six

Marc forced himself to look away, trying to ignore the tightness in his lower belly. "How did you get started in this kind of business?" he asked her casually, trying to distract his mind from the dangerous course it was taking. "Most people don't just wake up one morning and decide to go into the gourmet food business."

"Actually, that's just about exactly what did happen," Paige replied with a soft laugh. "When Peter died, he left me with a mountain of debts. I had no money, no job and nothing behind me but a degree in English—not the thing great careers are made of. I took an inventory of my skills and discovered there were two things I knew how to do really well: spend money and throw good parties. There didn't seem to be many openings for the first, but I parlayed my ability to plan parties into a very junior position in a catering company. I worked there for about a year, then decided to go out on my own. Toronto's overrun with catering companies and party planners, but there seemed to be room for this sort of thing.'' She smiled and gestured toward the enamel stockpot.

Marc nodded, watching her. Why? he found himself wondering. She'd grown up in wealth and luxury, and she and her son obviously hadn't been disinherited or tossed out of the family mansion. So why was she living in an old house she could barely afford, working fifteen-hour days just to hold things together? What had happened to make her so fiercely determined to succeed on her own? ''I'm impressed,'' he said quite truthfully.

She smiled dryly. ''That Harrington J. Pricefield's daughter can actually support herself and her son?'' It was so close to what he'd been thinking that Marc felt himself flush. Paige laughed merrily. ''It's all right—I'm used to it by now. All my friends think I'm crazy. The ones I still have, anyway.'' Then her smile faded and she looked down at the wine as she swirled it. ''I guess I'm trying to prove something.''

''I kind of figured that.''

''That obvious, huh?'' She smiled good-naturedly. Then she sighed. ''All my life, I've been taken care of. If I got into trouble, Daddy fixed it. I never had to take responsibility for anything I did or said. But all that changed when Peter died.'' She was silent for a moment. ''I married Peter without knowing anything about him except that he was handsome and exciting and rich. He lived in the fast lane: travel and parties, lots of high-powered business deals, the private jet, yacht, ski chalet in Switzerland. Daddy never liked him, but I just put that down to a typical father's belief that *no* man is good enough for his daughter.

"But when Peter died, I found out that his life had been an elaborate sham. He was just a wheeler and a dealer, always living on the edge, playing both ends against the middle. After the funeral, I discovered I was flat broke. Peter had borrowed against the house and property my parents had given us as a wedding gift, his life insurance, everything."

She gazed into her glass. "There was nothing left but a small computer company that was on the verge of bankruptcy. Peter had been buying and selling companies during those last few months in spite of the fact he didn't have a nickel in his pocket, using the profits from one to finance another. He'd created a paper empire, and when he died, it just collapsed. And a lot of people got hurt.

"Our lawyer spent weeks going over it all with me, trying to make me understand. He couldn't believe I could have been so ignorant of what had been going on." She looked up at Marc. "Money was something I'd never had to think about—it was just always there, like the air you breathe. I'll never forget the look of...of disgust on his face when he told me not to worry, that I could always run home to Daddy and let him clean up the mess. Suddenly I saw myself as he saw me—a rich, spoiled brat with no sense of responsibility. I never wanted anyone looking at me like that again!"

She drew in a deep breath. "All I had left was a

pile of debts—and the computer company. It had been successful before Peter had started draining it dry, and the employees thought it could be again. They wanted to buy it, but what they could pay wouldn't have covered even a tenth of what I owed. Then we got an offer in from a New York investor who was looking for a Canadian distributor for his own computers and software. He planned to shut down the manufacturing end of it and turn it into a retail outlet, putting more than 120 people out of work.'' Paige looked up at Marc, a glint of defiance in her velvet eyes. "I told him to go to hell. I sold everything that hadn't been repossessed and cashed in my grandmother's trust, paid off all my personal debts and had enough left over to cover one month's payroll. Then I sold the company to the employees for one dollar.'' She smiled faintly. "It was the first decent thing I'd done in my entire life—the first time I'd put someone else's needs ahead of my wants. I swore that from then on, I would make a life for myself I could be proud of. I didn't want Tyler growing up to be like his father, thinking the whole world was created merely for his entertainment.''

Marc realized he'd been holding his breath. He eased it out, staring down at her in amazement. "You are one hell of a remarkable woman, Paige Mac-Kenzie.''

She blushed. "I don't know what's in this wine— I don't usually dump all this on complete strangers. In fact, you're the first person I've ever talked to about it.''

Impulsively, Marc reached out and touched her

cheek. He ran his thumb delicately across her moist lips. She seemed to go very still, her eyes huge, locked with his, drawing him toward her. "I seem to have a knack for knocking down your walls, lady," he whispered hoarsely.

"Yes," she breathed. "Yes, you do...."

He was going to kiss her, Marc realized with faint surprise as he took the glass from her hand and set it aside. In spite of all his best intentions, in spite of the fact that he knew he should go back to his own side of the house before things got out of hand, he was going to kiss her. But it was too late for good intentions. He'd known this was going to happen sooner or later; he couldn't change the path of fate. He heard her indrawn breath as he slipped his arms around her, and then that wine-sweet mouth was under his and he lost all touch with reality.

She tasted as sweet as he'd known she would, her mouth opening tentatively to the delicate probe of his tongue. Her lips became malleable and warm, melting under his, and then he was inside, tasting the richness of her, feeling the wet silk of her tongue against his as she responded to his coaxing kiss. He felt a tremor run through her and tightened his arms to draw her fully against him, engulfed by a delicious woman's warmth and softness, breathing in the fragrance of her hair and skin. He'd fantasized about this moment for so long that his body responded instantly, the strength of his arousal so vital and urgent that he felt her start. He groaned, wanting to pull away but unable to comply with anything but that primitive need. He captured her tongue and drew it deeply, fiercely, into his own mouth and groaned again when she responded. She let her body melt against him, lifting onto her tiptoes to fit herself to him intimately. Gently, he pressed himself against her.

Her breath caught and she shivered violently, tearing her mouth from his and pressing her face into the hollow of his throat. "Please…" She sounded breathless and faint. "I don't understand this.…"

"We don't have to understand it. We just have to go with our feelings. Isn't that what you said?"

"But—"

He cut her protest off by the simple expediency of kissing her. He ran his tongue across her teeth, under her upper lip, his breath catching when she responded, hesitantly at first and then more and more eagerly. Panting, he drew his mouth from hers, kissing her throat, the hollow under her ear. "I want to make love to you. I haven't been able to think of anything else all day."

"Oh, Marc!" She trembled, turning her mouth so it was under his again, warm and eager and alive.

How Marc managed not to pull her down onto the floor then and there was beyond him. He was half wild with the taste and scent of her, and he knew instinctively what she'd feel like naked against him, could almost hear the soft, urgent cry she'd make as he lost himself in the sweetness of her body. It would be so easy, he thought, dazed. She was as ready for him as he was for her, both of them so caught up in the erotic fantasy of the unexpected that he had no doubt they'd bring each other to quick, volcanic satisfaction within minutes.

But that's not what he wanted, he realized with a wondering despair. And she wasn't the kind of woman who could make love on her kitchen floor with a man she scarcely knew and not regret it afterward. She was an incredibly alive and passionate woman and had held those passions in abeyance for too long. But if he rushed her into answering those needs before she was ready, she'd never forgive him. He didn't want her awkward and embarrassed every time their eyes met, hating him for having made it so easy, for seeing her vulnerable. And he didn't really want to have to face himself in the mirror every morning with that knowledge, either. He'd had a few quick, impersonal liaisons over the years, but he wasn't very proud of any of them. They'd left him physically sated but aching with some emotional emptiness he'd never fully understood. And he was just too old for that kind of self-abuse.

He buried his face in her hair, tightening his arms in a desperate embrace and going very still. "Don't move," he pleaded against her ear, squeezing his eyes shut. "Dear God, Paige, do me a favor and don't even breathe."

She didn't. As though knowing exactly how precariously he was balanced on the edge of the precipice, she stood very still. Slowly, the sweet tension started to leave him and he could breathe again, a deep ache settling within him that he knew would be there for a while. He sensed her begin to relax and he cradled her against him, feeling her heart hammering against his as though she'd just run the four-minute mile.

"I'm sorry," she said in a hoarse whisper. "I—I don't know what happened. I don't usually—"

"You know what happened," Marc whispered. "We both knew it was going to happen. It was just a matter of when."

"No." Then, softly: "Yes."

"It's going to happen again," Marc assured her huskily, starting to kiss the side of her throat. Her skin was as soft as flower petals, and he felt her shiver as he ran his tongue over it, tasting her.

"No." Paige said it very firmly, more for her own benefit than his. She was so light-headed she was afraid to let go of him in case she simply collapsed in a heap at his feet, and she didn't know whether the pounding in her ears was his heartbeat or hers. What in heaven's name was happening to her? she wondered desperately. She pulled away from him unsteadily, flushed and tousled. "No, Marc," she said very calmly, taking a deep breath. "It would be crazy for us to get involved. You know that. One of the unwritten laws of getting along with neighbors is not to have affairs with them."

Marc chuckled. His hands were warm and gentle as they stroked her back in slow, hypnotic circles. "It's going to be pretty hard to pretend this never happened, Paige. Or to pretend we don't want it to happen again."

She looked up at him in desperation, trying to ignore the erotic promise in his eyes. "It's impossible, Marc. We can't be—" she forced herself to say the word aloud "—lovers and neighbors, too. And besides, I hardly know you!" She managed a gasp of

laughter when she said it, hoping to defuse the tension
between them by making a joke of it. But inside, she
didn't feel like laughing at all. The suddenness of it,
the ease with which it had happened, left her stunned
and frightened. She'd been attracted to a man before—after all, she was normal and healthy and very
much alive. But feeling that delicious little frisson of
sexual attraction was one thing, actually acting on it
quite another.

Marc gave that throaty little chuckle again. He bent
down and kissed her gently on the mouth. "Good
night, Paige. And don't worry. We'll take it slow and
easy. I'm not in any rush."

"But..." Paige subsided, not knowing what to say.
She couldn't very well stand there and virtuously tell
him it had been a mistake and to leave her alone.
She'd turned to warm butter in his hands, and if it
hadn't been for some last-minute hesitancy on his
part, they'd be making love right now. "I'm not in
any rush either, Marc," she said quite truthfully.
"And in spite of—of what this may have looked like,
I'm not ready for any kind of relationship yet. I hope
you won't be offended when I tell you to forget it."

He didn't look offended at all. In fact, he looked
suspiciously self-satisfied as he brushed a tendril of
hair off her forehead and kissed her lightly. "I'll get
Greg and Vic back in here first thing tomorrow morning to get this wall put back together. Your car's out
front, by the way. T.K. says it shouldn't give you any
more trouble. He replaced the battery and points,
cleaned the carb, put in some new wiring and gave it
a tune-up."

"Thank you," she said, dazed. "I—I'll pay him for—"

"Forget it. He owed me a favor." He grinned ingenuously. "I'll put it on your tab—you're up to two jars of ginger jam now. And dinner. Next week sometime. I'll cook; you wash."

And then he was gone, leaving Paige staring numbly at the empty doorway, wondering how on earth her life had suddenly gotten so complicated.

Just how, Marc found himself wondering nearly three days later, had he let his life get so complicated? He gave his head a shake and sat down on the suspended slate hearth jutting out from the half-installed double-sided fireplace dividing living room from dining room. He'd intended to spend the summer doing some long-overdue navel-gazing, and instead had wound up halfway in love with a woman who didn't want anything to do with him. Not the smartest move he'd ever made.

And Paige MacKenzie, he reminded himself morosely, would undoubtedly agree. He sighed and planted his elbows on his knees, staring gloomily into the mug of cold breakfast coffee he was still holding cupped between his palms. What was the matter with him? He was handling this whole thing with the grace of a bull elephant in rut, starting with punching a hole through her living room wall and ending with that adolescent fumbling match in her kitchen the other evening.

"Real cool move, d'Angelo," he muttered disgustedly. For somebody who was supposed to be worldly and sophisticated, he was doing a great job of imitating a total jerk. He couldn't remember the last time he'd failed so spectacularly with a woman. Or had wanted so badly to succeed. "Old age," he grumbled miserably, staring down at the ginger cat stretched out between his feet. "We're a fine pair, aren't we, Bub? You've lost the urge, and I've lost the knack."

He swirled the cold coffee, then sighed again and set it aside. Was this what it was going to be like in another twenty years? Just an old man and an old cat trading reminiscences in front of the fire? He fumbled through his pockets, found a crumpled cigarette package and opened it. He had the cigarette in his mouth and was looking for a match before he realized what he was doing, and he flung the thing into the bare hearth with an oath.

"She's not the only woman in the world," he reminded himself for the fiftieth time. He glanced across the empty room at the telephone. It sat forlornly on the newly installed cobalt-blue carpet where he'd left it last night, the slim leather phone directory beside it. He'd tried. Last night he'd thumbed through that book and tried—had honestly tried—to call some of the women in it, determined to get Paige MacKenzie out of his mind once and for all.

Like nearly everything else he'd tried lately, it had been a dismal failure. He'd actually made two or three calls, only to trade small talk with no enthusiasm at all until he hung up without having asked for the date he'd called about in the first place. After a couple of calls, he'd simply sat there, leafing through the book, hoping to see a name that would send that familiar jolt of excitement through him. Nothing. He hadn't been able to think of one woman he wanted to spend the evening with, and had finally tossed the book aside and settled for Bub's companionship instead. "You're in pathetic shape," he growled, "when the only thing that turns you on is take-out Chinese food, an overweight cat and the latest bestseller."

And he had to thank Paige for that. He didn't know what it was about her, exactly, but she definitely hit a resonant note within him. Although it certainly didn't appear that he'd hit a matching one within her. He looked across the room at the hole in his wall. It was covered by a colorful Navaho blanket now, nailed there very firmly from Paige's side. It had appeared there three mornings ago as, he supposed, some kind of subtle message. In spite of himself, Marc had to smile. Subtle? More subtle than barbed wire and guard dogs, maybe, but only just. He hadn't seen much of her in the last few days. In fact, had he not known how busy she was, he would have sworn that she was actively avoiding him. Never a day went by when his side of the house wasn't filled with the tantalizing smells of ginger marmalade or spaghetti sauce or barbecue spices. How she kept up the exhausting pace, he didn't know. It would have killed most people. Or made them give up. A phrase, he suspected, that wasn't in Paige's vocabulary.

He stood up and stretched, then walked to the kitchen. "Well, Bub," he told the cat hurrying beside him, "I guess we should just take the message and stay out of her life." Something, he added to himself with a sinking feeling, that was going to be easier said than done. Because the truth was that he'd like nothing better than to become an integral and important part of Paige MacKenzie's life!

"...thirty-eight, thirty-nine, *forty*!" Paige put the last small decorative jar on the counter with a bang, then closed her eyes and stretched, massaging her aching lower back with both hands. Perspiration trickled down her temples, and she ran the back of her hand across her forehead, brushing back wet tendrils of hair that had escaped from her ponytail. She gazed down at the forty spice jars in relief. Thank goodness that was over! She hated grinding spices. Her own special blend of barbecue spice seemed to be a hit with everyone who tried it, but she still detested preparing it. No matter how careful she was, she always wound up with the kitchen and herself liberally powdered with the stuff, and she spent the next day or two reeking of cumin and chili peppers.

Behind her, a caldron of spaghetti sauce bubbled and steamed, adding more heat to the already stifling kitchen. The aromas of garlic and tomato sauce blended with the pungent tang of spices that still hung in the air, but Paige scarcely noticed them. She hurriedly estimated how many jars the sauce would yield. Twenty, if she was lucky. Chiaro's Food Emporium wanted twice that, but they'd have to take what she had. The catch was that they wanted the sauce tomorrow morning as part of a display for International Food Week. In the meantime, she would label these bottles of spices and the sixty jars of ginger marmalade lined up on the dining room table, deliver them, then race back and sterilize, fill, seal and label the jars of spaghetti sauce. Then there was the peach chutney for Charley's Deli.

Poor Tyler. She'd promised to take him out to the zoo today, but that was impossible now. Maybe tomorrow...

Her palms felt clammy, and Paige took a deep breath, fighting the feeling of panicky desperation that had been growing steadily stronger all morning. She felt as though she were drowning, as though every time she got her head above water and tried to take a breath, another wave would come crashing down on top of her. Cabbages and Kings had phoned that morning, asking about the order of ginger marmalade she'd promised them three days ago. The owner of Lady Jane Boutique had called to say that if Paige couldn't fill her orders, they'd be forced to go elsewhere. The Church Street Deli had called twice now about the tarragon vinegar she'd rashly promised them last week.

Then there were the bills. She looked numbly at the stack of envelopes on the end of the counter. Bills for jars, for labels, for the advertising flyers that were still sitting on the coffee table because she hadn't had time to mail them. There were the regular bills, too: telephone, heat, water, car, credit card, house insurance, taxes. At the word "taxes," Paige's stomach gave a twist and she thought of the other letter that had come yesterday, the one from the tax department telling her that her home had been reassessed. Her municipal taxes had just doubled, it had advised her

calmly, and she had until the month's end to come
up with twelve hundred dollars or be considered in
arrears.

Just thinking about it made her feel sick. She had
exactly twenty-two hundred dollars in the bank as of
that morning. And unless something dramatic happened between now and the month's end, she was
going to lose everything. GingerBread Preserves.
Chestnut Manor. Any dream she'd ever had of making it on her own.

She swallowed. She had to talk to the bank about
a small-business loan; that was all there was to it.
She'd sit down and work out a calm, detailed presen-
tation, listing her assets, her market evaluation, copies
of her long-term orders, estimates of expenses and
income. If she just took a logical and businesslike
approach, they'd see her side. She was a good risk.
She'd already proved she made a good product. And
she'd proved she could go out and sell it, too. In fact,
she had more orders than she could fill. That would
convince them, if nothing else did! She just needed
to get her feet solidly under her and the money would
start pouring in.

Paige took a deep breath, firming her resolve. Right
now, she told herself. She'd call the bank right now
and make an appointment with the loans manager.
There was just no other way. Just having made the
decision seemed to calm her. With some money in
the bank, she could face anything.

Except, of course, Marc d'Angelo.

He was driving her crazy. That was the only explanation. She hadn't been able to think of anything

else for three solid days, her mind filled with the memory of his lazy blue eyes, the sound of his husky laughter, those delirious minutes in his arms the other night. Every now and again she'd catch an unexpected scent of that leathery cologne he wore or she'd glance up and see him padding through her house on some errand or another, his rugged features frowning and preoccupied. Every time their eyes met she felt as though her heart would stop altogether. Finally, she'd simply started avoiding him. It was easier that way. Although there were times when she wondered why she didn't just take that blanket down and let nature take its course!

Because you're a coward, she admitted. You're scared silly of losing your heart to that man. Probably with reason, she added grudgingly. It would be easy to fall in love right now. Or at least *think* she was in love. She was vulnerable and alone and scared to death most of the time; falling in love, turning her heart and her life over to someone else, would be all too easy. And she'd fought too long and too hard to take the easy way out now. Sorry, Marc, she told him silently. But I've got to get through this on my own.

Somehow. Paige took another deep breath. She had no choice. She'd get through this day somehow. And the days to follow. One by one, until she had both Chestnut Manor *and* GingerBread Preserves licked.

"But, Mommy, you promised!" Tyler's voice wavered.

"Tyler, I know I promised to take you to the zoo, but I can't!" Paige tried to keep the rising impatience out of her voice. "Honey, I'll take you tomorrow. But right now Mommy's very busy." *Busy,* Paige thought a little hysterically. Panic-stricken was more like it! How in heaven's name was she going to get everything done?

"Don't wanna go tomorrow," Tyler was sobbing, clutching his blanket. Chin wobbling, he stared up at her miserably, tear-filled eyes mirroring anger and disappointment. "You promised!"

"Oh, Tyler." Paige felt her own eyes start to burn. He looked so small and forlorn standing there, shirt misbuttoned and only half tucked into his brown corduroy pants, jacket tucked under one arm in anticipation. He'd been so good today, playing quietly by himself while she'd been busy, that her last-minute betrayal was doubly unfair. "I promise we'll go tomorrow. We'll spend the whole afternoon there, okay?"

"Don't wanna go tomorrow!" he wailed, stamping his foot. "You said today. You said—"

"Tyler, I know what I said!" The words came out more sharply than she'd intended. Tyler gave an even louder howl, the trickle of tears turned to an all-out torrent.

Bub sauntered into the kitchen just then, his rolling stride and muscled build making him look for all the world like a dockside tough who'd wandered in to quiet things down. He stared at Tyler, tail twitching slightly, then swung his blazing golden eyes onto Paige.

"Get out of here," she said to the cat angrily. "Tyler, stop it! We'll go tomorrow. That's the best I can do. And if you're going to throw a tantrum, go to your room."

Paige could have sworn the old cat growled. Its stare burned into her accusingly, seeming to hold her personally responsible for the unhappiness in Tyler's young life. "I told you to get out of here," she hissed at it. Ignoring an urge to drop everything and gather her heartbroken son up into her arms, Paige turned away abruptly. Tyler's howls rose in volume. "Tyler, I said stop it!" She slammed her palm down onto the counter so hard the phone on the end jangled.

Tyler jumped, staring up at her through streaming tears. Then, pausing only long enough to drag in a deep, fortifying breath, he started to cry even harder, stamping both feet in frustrated anger. Then he turned and ran.

"Tyler, I'm sorry!" Paige made a grab for him, but he slipped through her hands and headed for the living room. Bub gave a startled snarl and bolted after him, nearly tripping her, and she swore at him. "Tyler...!" She stopped, staring after him in defeat. "Oh, damn it," she whispered, pressing her fingers against her forehead to stop her own tears from spilling. "Tyler, I'm sorry." Shoulders drooping with exhaustion and misery, she turned back to the kitchen. Let him cry it out for a while, she told herself. Heaven knew he had a right to be furious and hurt. She'd make it up to him tomorrow. And maybe, if she had time, she'd take him out for a hamburger tonight as a peace offering.

She glanced guiltily toward the empty door, then sighed and reached for the unopened box of custom-printed labels she'd picked up the day before. One step at a time, she reminded herself. She'd label the spice and marmalade now, then deliver them. By the time she got back, the spaghetti sauce would be finished and she could fill the jars and seal them, then clean up the kitchen a bit and get started on the peach chutney. If everything went smoothly, she'd be finished by midnight. One o'clock at the latest.

Seven

By the time Marc had cleaned the paint off his hands and set the brushes to soak, Tyler had all but stopped crying. He sat on a kitchen chair, stubby little legs stuck straight out, face still flushed and wet, and he gave an occasional hiccup as he gnawed at an oatmeal cookie. He looked, Marc decided, like the saddest little boy in the world. Even Bub seemed concerned, sitting on the floor in front of him, purring like a chain saw, ever watchful for stray crumbs.

"Feeling better?" Marc kneeled by the chair and wiped the small face with a damp cloth. Tyler nodded. "Okay, let's pop through the hole and let your mom know where you are."

"Don't wanna go home," Tyler said decisively. "I wanna stay here wif you and Bub."

"Oh, boy." Marc took a deep breath and stood up.

"You've got to give your mom a chance, Tyler. I know you're mad at her, but let's go hear her side of the story, okay?"

"No." Tyler's voice and expression made it clear that he had no interest in reconciliation.

"Oh, boy," Marc repeated, blowing his cheeks out. Now what?

"Hey, big brother." Greg wandered in just then, wiping plaster dust off his bare shoulders and torso with a crumpled T-shirt. He grabbed a handful of cookies from the open bag and perched on the table, ruffling Tyler's hair as he walked by. "I'm taking the rest of the afternoon off to catch the Jays-Red Sox game with Gabe and Pop. You coming?"

Marc shook his head, then looked around at Greg. "How about taking Tyler? He's had a pretty bad day. A baseball game and a couple of hot dogs might make him feel better."

"Sure." Greg took off his Blue Jays cap and dropped it on Tyler's head. "You a Jays fan, sport?"

"Just don't fill him so full of junk food that he gets sick," Marc cautioned. "I don't want his mother coming after me with a hatchet."

"Any special time you want him back?" Greg asked with a broad grin. "I'd hate to walk in on anything."

Marc gave Greg a look of sublime disgust. "This isn't part of some adolescent seduction scene, Lothario. I'll leave that to you young studs. I'm just being a nice guy and getting Tyler out of his mom's hair for a while. And vice versa."

"Uh-huh." Greg smiled disbelievingly. He slid off

the table and kneeled to button Tyler's shirt properly and tuck it in, then zipped up his jacket. Tyler stood still, wrinkling his nose when Greg dusted cookie crumbs off his mouth and chin. "Okay, buddy. Let's go to a ball game." Tyler gave a squeal of laughter as Greg swept him up onto his shoulders. "Have fun, big brother. And don't do anything I wouldn't."

"That leaves enough options to get me thirty years to life," Marc muttered. He looked at the clock, then drew in a deep, fortifying breath. "Guess I'd better get over there and tell her where Tyler is," he told the old cat. "Before she sends out the SWAT team."

The mouth-watering aroma of garlic, onions and spices engulfed Marc as he walked into Paige's kitchen, and he sniffed appreciatively. He wandered over to the stove and peered into the big pot, then took a spoon out of the nearest drawer and helped himself to a sample. "Good."

"What?"

Paige's startled query made Marc smile. Still licking the spoon clean, he strolled into the dining room. She was sitting at the table, up to her elbows in a clutter of jam and spices, labels, pens, tape. She looked hot and very tired, tendrils of hair pasted to her wet forehead, her cheeks flushed. "I said, your spaghetti sauce is good. Needs a little more basil maybe, but it's not a bad effort for a WASP."

She dabbed glue on a label with abrupt, angry motions. "That's really what I need right now, a racist food critic!"

"I'm not being racist. It's not your fault you

weren't born Italian." Marc grinned. "You manage pretty well in spite of the handicap."

"Oh...go away!"

There was something in her voice that Marc could have sworn was a sob. He frowned and looked more closely at her. Her eyes were very bright and had the wild, desperate look of something trapped, and she seemed to be struggling to hold herself in control. "Hey," he said softly. "Are you all right?"

"Yes!" Then, to Marc's utter astonishment, she burst into tears. "No, I'm not all right!" she wailed. "I've got twenty jars of spaghetti sauce to put up by tonight and I was supposed to take Tyler to the zoo but I can't and now he's mad at me and I have to deliver all this jam and now these labels won't stick!" She threw the glue bottle down, sending labels flying in all directions. "They sent me the wrong ones! Five hundred labels, and not one of them has any glue on it!"

"Oh, God." Marc groaned. He gazed down at her, torn between an urge to laugh and an even stronger one to gather her into his arms and comfort her as he had Tyler a few minutes ago. Just what was it about these two, he asked himself wearily, that brought out the protective instinct in him? "Come on." He took her hand and drew her to her feet. "Time for a break."

"I can't," she hiccuped, dabbing at her nose with the tissue he handed her. "I've got so much to do...."

"It'll wait," Marc told her gruffly, untying her apron and tossing it aside. He wiped a dusting of ginger off the end of her nose, then slid his arm around her shoulders and gently escorted her into the living room. "You're asleep on your feet. When was the last time you took a day off?"

"Can't afford to." She followed as he led her toward the sofa. "I'm too busy."

"Sit." Marc gave her a gentle push and she just folded up and collapsed onto the deep-cushioned sofa. "You're running yourself ragged. Keep this pace up and you're not going to be any good to yourself, your son *or* GingerBread Preserves."

To his surprise, she didn't argue. He ducked over to his side of the house, and when he came back she was still sitting there, dabbing at her nose and eyes. He put the whiskey glass in her hands and she stared at it. "Drink it," he ordered. "All of it." He lifted it to her lips and she took a deep swallow, nearly gagging when the Scotch hit the back of her throat.

Five minutes later, she was sound asleep. Marc slipped the glass out of her hand and set it on the table, then swung her feet up and tucked one of the cushions under her head. He found a blanket in an upstairs closet and draped it over her, then brushed a handful of thick, tangled hair off her face and stared down at her for a thoughtful moment. In sleep, she looked like a child herself, the perpetual worry lines between her brows erased, mouth relaxed into a near smile. He found himself smiling as he bent down impulsively and kissed her forehead. Then, sighing heavily, he walked back into the dining room. It was, he decided as he sat down and reached for the glue bottle and the first label, going to be a long day.

* * *

It took Paige a full minute to figure out where she was when she woke up. She rubbed her eyes and gazed around sleepily. Marc was sprawled in the big chair across from her, one long leg thrown over the arm, engrossed in a magazine. A beer bottle and an empty plate sat on the floor beside him, and Paige wondered why seeing him there, perfectly at home in *her* house, didn't annoy her as much as it should have. Probably, she decided, because she was so used to having him underfoot that she sort of missed him when he wasn't. It was almost frightening, the easy way he'd made himself part of her life. And even more frightening, the way she'd accepted it.

Marc glanced up just then. He smiled and stretched lazily, letting the magazine fall closed. "I was beginning to think you were out for the count. Hungry?"

"Starved. How long was I asleep?"

"About seven hours."

"Seven...hours?" Paige stared at him disbelievingly. "Oh, my God! The jam!" She kicked her feet free of the blanket and struggled to sit up. "Why did you let me sleep so long! Tyler must be starved, and I have to get the jam over to—"

"Relax. Tyler's fine, and I delivered the jam hours ago." Marc eased himself to his feet. He picked up the bottle and plate and headed toward the kitchen. "And I dropped that barbecue spice off at the Church Street Deli while I was at it. That was who it was for, wasn't it? That scruffy little note you have taped to the fridge wasn't a lot of help."

"*You* delivered the jam?" She turned to look at his retreating back. "But the labels—"

"Glued on good and solid," he assured her from the kitchen. "You like hot mustard on your pastrami, or regular?"

"Hot," she replied absently.

He came back in a few minutes with a plate stacked high with a pastrami sandwich on light rye, a bottle of beer and a glass of milk. He pushed the coffee table in front of Paige and set the sandwich and milk on it, then settled back into the chair again, balancing the beer on his thigh.

"Thank you. For everything." Paige smiled a trifle ruefully and reached for the sandwich. "You must be wondering how I ever managed to take care of myself before I met you."

"The thought's crossed my mind."

Paige looked up, her mouth full of pastrami.

Marc held her gaze steadily. "I'm beginning to think you need someone to take care of you, lady. Because you're sure not doing a very good job of it yourself." Paige gave an indignant sputter, trying to swallow and protest at the same time, but Marc ignored her. He planted his elbows on his knees and leaned forward. "You're driving yourself too hard, Paige. You're trying to be the best at everything—but this isn't a damned contest. Can't you see that? You're wearing yourself out. And you're wearing me out looking after you."

Paige licked mustard off her lower lip, eyeing Marc over the raised sandwich. "I don't remember hiring you as my guardian angel. You didn't have to spend the day gluing jam labels and making my deliveries, you know."

"It's not just today!" He lunged to his feet, making an all-encompassing gesture with the beer bottle. "It's every day, Paige. It's this house, your parents—even Tyler." He stared down at her, face and eyes impatient. "When was the last time you spent an hour just relaxing with your son? Have you even talked with him today? Aside from that brawl you had about the zoo?"

His words hit a little too close to home. Paige felt herself flush. She set the sandwich down carefully and wiped her hands on the paper napkin he'd provided. "I don't think my relationship with my son is any of your business," she said calmly, carefully avoiding his eyes.

"It is when he comes running to me for sympathy."

Paige's head shot up. She looked around the room swiftly, then back at Marc, eyes narrowing. "What do you mean, he went running to you for sympathy? And where is he?"

"He popped over to my side of the wall about two this afternoon, upset at life in general and you in particular. Greg took him to the baseball game. They should be back soon."

"That wasn't necessary," Paige told him icily. "Tyler understands what—"

"Like hell he understands!" Marc glared down at her in exasperation. "He's a four-year-old kid, for crying out loud."

"I'm well aware of that."

"Are you?" Marc asked brutally. "And are you also 'well aware' that he's growing up fast? That pretty soon he's going to be all grown up, and you'll have missed it all?''

Guilt, as familiar and painful as an old toothache, jolted through Paige. Somehow she managed to hold Marc's impatient stare, praying he couldn't see her feelings in her eyes. "Look, I don't need anyone telling me how to raise my son."

"No?" he asked bluntly. "Tyler needs a mother, Paige, not an overworked, short-tempered woman who's pushing herself so hard she's missing all the magic of her son's childhood. You're trying so hard to be your own woman that you're not leaving enough of yourself for anyone else."

The instant the words were out of his mouth, Marc knew he'd gone too far. He saw anger flare in her eyes, and under it, the raw hurt. He stepped toward her, opening his mouth to apologize when he realized it was too late for that, too. Damn it, why couldn't he keep his mouth shut? He wheeled away from her, as angry at himself as at her, and angrier at life in general than at either. Damn Peter MacKenzie, he thought as he stalked across to the hole in the wall. And damn Harrington J. Pricefield, too. And all the other bits and pieces of her past that had conspired to bring her to this point, working herself into exhaustion trying to make a life for herself and her son that wasn't made up of lies.

He swept the Navaho blanket aside roughly and eased himself through the ragged hole into his own side of the house. That's it, he told himself savagely. You're going to stay the hell out of her life from here on in. You're just making a bad time worse for her.

She said it herself: She doesn't need any more aggravation.

He was dozing on the sofa when Greg came in. He opened one bleary eye and looked up at his brother, then sat up with a groan and scrubbed his face with his hands. Greg grinned. "You disappoint me, big brother. At the very least, I figured dim lights, a romantic little fire, a bottle of wine…" He left it hanging, his grin broadening at Marc's look. Then he nodded at the sleeping child cradled in his arms. "Little guy's got a lot of stamina, but he gave out halfway through the eighth inning."

Marc gave a groaning laugh when he looked at Tyler. The baseball cap was still perched on the boy's fair head, and he had one small, grubby fist clenched around a blue and white pennant. He wore only one sneaker, and his shirt and face were almost unrecognizable under the colorful layers of cherry soda, mustard and dirt. But even in sleep, his mouth was curved in an utterly blissful smile.

Gently, Marc eased him out of Greg's arms and cradled him against his shoulder. Greg pried the missing sneaker out of his hip pocket and handed it to Marc, then said good-night and left.

Paige was still sitting on the sofa when Marc maneuvered himself and Tyler through the hole in the wall. She was curled up in the far corner, her arms locked around her updrawn knees, forehead resting on them. She looked up when he stepped into her living room, and the instant their eyes locked, Marc realized she'd been crying.

His mouth tightened and he looked away. Paige

untangled her legs and stood up, furtively wiping her cheek with the back of her hand as she walked toward him, eyes downcast, looking very subdued.

"I'll take him up for you," Marc said gruffly, starting up the stairs. To his surprise, she didn't argue. She padded up the stairs after him and followed him to Tyler's room, watching silently as he laid the sleeping boy on the bed. "Do you have a wet cloth?" He looked around. She was standing by the door, silhouetted against the light from the hallway, arms tightly crossed under her small breasts in a protective gesture he doubted she was even aware of. "His hands and face are pretty dirty."

Her wide dark eyes met his, held them for a taut moment. Then she nodded and turned away, and Marc realized he'd been holding his breath. He released it in a noisy, resigned sigh, then gently pried Tyler's sticky fingers from around the pennant stick. He set it on the maple bedside table where Tyler would see it first thing in the morning, then tugged the cap off the mop of tangled golden curls and laid it on top. "Come on, sport, let's get this jacket off." As Marc eased him out of his jacket, Tyler frowned and whimpered softly but didn't waken.

"You do that very well, Mr. d'Angelo." Paige stepped around to the other side of the bed, her back rigid, eyes defiant. "You're really all things to all people, aren't you? Bricklayer, plumber, carpenter. Adopted father."

The hostility in her voice was raw. Marc looked up at her sharply and then, suddenly, understanding dawned. Of course! He cursed himself silently. Why hadn't he anticipated this? Tyler was the most precious thing in her precarious life, the only thing that made any sense, that gave her stability and ballast in a world gone a little mad. And she'd fight like a tiger to keep anything—or anyone—from coming between them.

"Paige…"

"I can take over now, thank you," she said precisely, sitting on the opposite side of the bed. She started wiping the grime gently from Tyler's sleeping face, not looking at Marc. "Thank your brother for me when you see him. It was thoughtful of him to take Tyler to the game. But in the future, I'd appreciate it if you'd stay away from my son. I realize you thought you were being kind, but it's confusing for him to have two adults to listen to, two sets of rules. He's very vulnerable at the moment, and I don't want him attaching himself to you, then being hurt. He's had enough hurt in his life so far."

And so have you, Marc told her silently, reading the pain and fear and vulnerability on her face as though the words themselves were printed there. He found himself wanting to wrap his arms around her to scare out whatever demons lurked back there in the shadows of her mind. Impulsively, he reached out and caught her hand. She flinched as though burned and tried to pull free, but he braided his fingers with hers firmly.

"Listen to me, Paige," he said quietly. "I'm not trying to play father to your son. And I'm not trying to undercut your authority with him or use him to get to you somehow. The boy was upset and disappointed this afternoon. You were at the end of your tether. Greg was going to the game, and I figured you and Tyler could use a break from each other. That's all there was to it. I know I stepped way out of bounds, and I'm sorry for that. But I'm not sorry for making a little boy happy for a few hours, or for giving his mother some breathing space.''

Paige stared at him uncertainly, wanting to believe him, to trust him, but afraid to. The eyes that held hers were so deeply blue in the faint light coming from the hallway that they were almost black. And then, abruptly, all the tension and anger went out of her. He hadn't been trying to compete for Tyler's affections; she knew that. She'd just been lashing out, trying to assuage some of her own guilt and hurt by inflicting some on him.

Her shoulders sagged and she closed her eyes, nodding. ''I'm sorry,'' she whispered. ''I—I know why you did it. I just get a little protective sometimes.'' Then she looked up, smiling ruefully. ''That's an understatement, isn't it? It's just that he usually doesn't like strangers, especially men. This is the first time I've seen him take to someone so quickly, and I was afraid that...'' She shrugged, letting her gaze slide from his. Afraid of what? she asked herself. Afraid of losing your son to this tall, blue-eyed man or of becoming so inextricably entangled with him yourself that you'll never fight your way free?

''Don't apologize for loving your son,'' Marc told her softly. ''You've got one of the hardest jobs in the world. And so far, I'd say you were doing pretty okay.''

Paige looked up at him, surprised by his frank approval. And inexplicably pleased by it as well. "Thank you," she murmured. "And anytime you want…well, I mean I don't mind you and your brothers playing with Tyler. Some rowdy male companionship now and again will do him some good." She had to laugh then, and wrinkled her nose expressively. "He must get awfully tired of having no one to play with but his mother."

Marc laughed quietly. "Oh, I suspect his mother's just about the most important person in his life. And understandably," he added, holding her gaze, "because she's fast becoming a pretty important person in mine, too."

It caught Paige so by surprise that she couldn't think of a thing to say in reply. She felt the heat of a blush pour across her cheeks and found herself wondering inanely why every time she was near this man she turned into an idiot. But Marc didn't seem to notice. He gave her fingers a gentle squeeze, then took the wet facecloth and wiped a smear of mustard from Tyler's chin.

"You ought to have one or two of your own," she ventured after a moment. "You're a natural at this."

"Someday." He glanced at her, smiling. "Gabe and his wife have a new baby, and I have two married sisters with five kids between them."

Paige's eyes widened. "Just how many of you *are* there, anyway?"

"Starting at the top, there's Roman, Maria, Gabriel, me, Angelica, Victor and Gregorio."

"Seven," she said almost wistfully. "It must be nice, having lots of brothers and sisters."

"It is now that I'm old enough to appreciate it. But there were times when I was growing up that I'd have given anything to have been an only child. I had to share my parents with six other kids, three older and three younger. There was never any privacy, and you couldn't keep anything secret. It was like growing up in a college dorm."

Paige smiled. "But I'll bet you always had someone to play with."

Marc laughed aloud. "Yeah, that was never a problem." He looked at her teasingly. "But I'll bet you never had to wear hand-me-downs. And I'll bet you always got the corner piece of the cake even when it wasn't your birthday—the one with all the icing on it."

It was Paige's turn to laugh. "No, and yes." Then she sighed, brushing a sweep of hair off Tyler's forehead. "But I'll bet your parents found it easier to let you go when it was time, to let you grow up. You weren't all they had." She stroked Tyler's cheek with the back of her hand, thinking of Vincenzo d'Angelo. She'd watched the older man work with his sons over the past few days, and she was touched at the uncomplicated pride he took in everything they did. He had a gruff, sometimes impatient manner, but he always listened attentively when they had something to say and treated their suggestions and even their complaints with respect.

"He loves you. You know that, don't you?" Marc said.

"Daddy?" Paige looked up, surprised to discover him standing beside her. She smiled. "Yes, I know. That's why I feel so guilty when I get angry with him. I suspect all this has been harder on him than it's been on me. It's always harder to watch someone walk a tightrope than to do it yourself."

"He'll come around." Marc rammed his hands into the hip pockets of his jeans and nudged an overturned toy truck with his toe. "Look, Paige, about this afternoon…"

"Don't say it." Paige stood up and pulled the sheet and light blanket up over Tyler, tucking them under the sleeping boy's chin. She straightened, keeping her back to Marc, and stared down at her son. "You didn't say a thing I didn't need to hear. I know I've been a terrible mother to Tyler these last few months. I keep telling myself that it's just going to be for a little while, that once I get things under control I'll be able to hire some help and make it up to him. But none of that makes me feel less guilty. That's why I got mad at you. Because you were telling me the truth, and it hurt."

"Paige…" He cupped her shoulders gently. "I was way out of line today. I have no right judging you."

"Oh, Marc!" Paige wheeled toward him blindly and buried herself in his fierce embrace. His arms folded around her tightly, and she slipped her own arms around his narrow waist and hugged him desperately, tears suddenly filling her eyes. "Sometimes I get so confused and scared! Some days I think I'm going to lose it all, that it's going to get away from me and run me right into the ground."

His hands moved in comforting circles on her back, strong and competent. "It's all right, Paige," he murmured against her ear. "It's not going to get away from you. You're too strong for that."

"It just goes on and on and never stops," she sobbed quietly. "And I feel so guilty all the time. About Tyler, about Daddy, about all the orders I mess up or can't deliver. I feel as though I'm on a treadmill and someone keeps speeding it up." She drew in a deep, shuddering breath, swallowing tears, and clenched her eyes closed. "Hold me. Please, just hold me."

"For as long as you need," Marc whispered.

His breath was warm and moist on her throat. Paige turned toward it instinctively, and then his mouth was on hers and she was kissing him with a desperate intensity, tasting him, wanting him. He groaned deep in his throat and ran his hands up into her tangled mane of hair, cupping her head and tipping it back as his mouth possessed hers with unbridled hunger.

And Paige answered that hunger with her own, letting the riptide of passion and raw desire sweep her under. There was neither beginning nor end to it, nothing but the all-powerful urgency of *now*, of being in this man's arms and wanting him so badly she ached with it. His mouth played with hers, nibbling, coaxing, and she teased back, gently biting the sensuous swell of his lower lip, touching the tip of her tongue to his and coaxing it deeply into her mouth, then pulling away to nip at his chin, his lips.

There was no holding back this time, no hesitancy. It was as though they'd already passed the point of question and answer, Paige thought dimly. As though all the awkward preliminaries had already been taken care of in the locked glances and shy smiles and moments of laughter they'd traded during the last few days. She shivered lightly and let her head fall back to bare her throat to his marauding mouth, feeling herself go warm and weak as he nuzzled the collar of her denim shirt aside to get at the tender place at the curve of her shoulder.

He ran his hand down her shoulder, then down still farther to her breast, stroking his flattened palm lightly over the nipple until it went pebble hard. An electric warmth shot through her, arrowing from breast to loin, and Paige gave a tiny moan of pleasure so explicit it made Marc catch his breath. He slipped the top buttons of her shirt open and pushed it and her bra straps off her shoulders, then buried his face in the sweet cleft between her breasts with a groan of satisfaction. His tongue lapped at her, slid under the lace trim of her bra, darted here and there until Paige had to bite her lip to keep from crying out. She sank her fingers into his thick hair and arched her back, her eyes closing in anticipation as he pushed the lacy edge of her bra back.

"Marc..." His name caught in her throat, and she had to fight to catch her breath, a silken warmth flooding through her as his tongue found the budding nipple and started teasing it. "Oh, Marc, yes!"

Marc murmured something and nuzzled more material aside, his tongue warm and wet as it laved the underside of her breast, circled the nipple, ran slowly upward again until his mouth was on hers and he was kissing her with deep and unhurried delight. He ran his hands up and down her back, molding her to him. Paige caught her breath as he slipped one hand under the waistband of her corduroy jeans, his palm gliding slowly down the outward flare of her spine, lifting and holding her against him. Then his coaxing hand was under the filmy fabric of her briefs, cupping the lush fullness of her bottom, and Paige gave a soft whimper that Marc silenced as his mouth covered hers hungrily.

But in spite of Marc's caution, Tyler half wakened. He stirred behind them, mumbling something sleepily, and Marc eased Paige away from him regretfully. "I don't think it's the time or the place to continue this," he murmured. "He's a pretty together sort of kid, but I don't know what it would do to his psyche to wake up and find some strange man making love to his mother on his bedroom floor."

Paige gave a soft, breathless laugh and glanced at her son. He was still asleep, his face sweetly innocent in a beam of moonlight. "Actually, he'd probably approve." She looked back at Marc. "He's crazy about you."

Marc's gaze locked with hers. "And how does his mother feel?"

Paige's heart gave a thump. She felt drawn into those indigo eyes, knowing he could read the answer on her face, in her eyes. Knowing that he wanted her to say it. "She's crazy about you, too," she whispered.

"Paige." He whispered her name with something nearing reverence, his eyes caressing her face feature by feature. Then he kissed her, lightly at first, then more and more deeply. His breath was slightly unsteady when he finally lifted his lips from hers. "I'd better go," he murmured. "Because if I don't go soon, I'm not going to go at all...."

"You don't have to go." Paige listened to her words as she might to a stranger's, her heart pounding. Marc's eyes held hers searchingly and she took a deep breath. "My bedroom is just down the hall."

"Paige..." He said it almost warningly, his fingers tightening on her shoulders as though physically keeping himself from crushing her against him. "Honey, you have to be sure about this. I'm past the age where I'm just looking for one-nighters. I don't want to be just a part of your self-discovery, part of the new Paige MacKenzie's growing process. I'm going to expect some kind of commitment."

"You mean you want to marry me and take over my half of Chestnut Manor?" Paige teased him.

He gave her a lopsided grin. "Yeah, something like that."

Paige touched his mouth with her fingers. "Marc, I'm twenty-seven years old. I have a four-year-old son and a business I'm barely keeping above water. I'm scared to death most of the time, and there are lots of days when I don't feel very grown-up. But if we make love tonight, you'll be the second man I've ever slept with in my entire life. And I was married to the first. There's never been anyone else. I don't know if that means I'm ready to make a commitment or not, because I hardly know what I'm going to be doing myself from one day to the next and a 'long-term plan' is one covering the next three days. But I do know that I'm no more interested in one-night stands than you are. For Tyler's sake, as well as mine. I don't want a succession of men going through his life any more than I want them going through mine. So maybe…maybe that's kind of a commitment in itself.''

Gazing down into that small upturned face, Marc felt his heart miss a beat. Commitment? he asked himself with awe. He'd asked for the moon and she'd given him the entire universe! She offered him not only her own heart but that of her son, and the trust implicit in that took his breath away. I love you, he whispered in his mind. He had his mouth open to say it aloud, then caught himself. It was too soon. For both of them. The words were easy to say tonight, with his mouth still sweet with the taste of her and her eyes filled with the promise of lovemaking. The words were always easy to say at times like this. But if he said them to this woman, he had to mean them. She didn't deserve anything less than the utter truth. And until he could be sure of that truth, and of his own heart, he wouldn't say anything at all.

She reached out her hand, almost shyly. Marc smiled and meshed his fingers tightly with hers. ''Sure?''

''Absolutely,'' she whispered.

They didn't say anything as they walked hand in hand down the hall and into the cool stillness of her bedroom. Somehow, without words, they'd said it all. There was a moment or two of awkwardness once they were actually in the room, but Marc had anticipated that and simply tugged her into his arms.

She stiffened for a fraction of an instant, then relaxed against him, her soft laugh muffled by his shirt. "All of a sudden I ran out of brave. Now what?"

Marc chuckled, feeling her heart race against his. "Now we just take it slow and easy. And if you have second thoughts anywhere along the line, just say so and we'll go back to being neighbors and forget all about this."

She was silent for so long that Marc wondered if she was going to do just that, finding himself torn between savage disappointment and relief. Maybe it would be better for both of them if she did, he brooded. Maybe he wasn't quite as ready as he'd thought for all that stability and commitment he'd been talking about. Maybe...

"No second thoughts," she whispered, looking up at him. Her eyes were wide and a little frightened. "I keep thinking I should, just for appearances, but I can't find even one."

"Good," he breathed, realizing even as he said it that he'd never been more certain about anything in his life. As he bent his head to kiss her, he caught a glimpse of Bub from the corner of one eye. He was standing in the hall, watching them, and just before Marc reached out with his left foot and pushed the door closed, he could have sworn he saw the old cat smile.

Eight

The door didn't quite close and a sliver of light from the hall lamp cut a golden swath across the carpet and bed. Marc gazed down into Paige's upturned face, feeling his heart start to pound as her eyes locked with his. They were slightly hooded and smoky with desire, and when she reached out and started to slowly unbutton his shirt, he wet his lips, his breathing suddenly shallow and fast.

Marc started undressing her, not allowing himself to actually touch her as he slipped her shirt off and tossed it away, wanting to draw out the anticipation as long as he could. He heard her breath catch as he unclasped her bra, but still he held himself back. Her breasts were small and high and firm, and he ached to fill his hands with their sweet heaviness, to feel the

nipples harden in his palms, to hear her gentle moans
as he stroked and caressed the sensitive flesh.

She'd finished unbuttoning his shirt and had tugged
it out of his jeans when he started pulling down the
zipper of her slacks. She clutched the fabric of his
gaping shirt with both hands and went motionless,
eyes closed, hardly breathing as he eased them down
over her slender hips and legs. He felt her tremble as
she lifted first one foot free, then the other, until she
was standing all but naked in the dark. Still kneeling
in front of her, Marc let his gaze run over her greedily, his breath catching at the perfection of her. Hers
was a woman's body, not that of a gawky girl, a
mother's body that still held the faint marks of the
child she'd borne. It imbued her with a delicious female lushness that he found incredibly erotic, and he
felt his body, already aching for her, respond so
strongly he had to catch his breath with the near pain
of it.

He cupped his hands on her waist and ran his palms
slowly down the flare of her hips, sliding his fingers
under the lacy band of her panties and easing them
down. He felt her muscles tighten as he ran his fingertips down the backs of her thighs and smiled at
her sudden sweet shyness. She took a quick breath as
he started kissing the soft, feminine swell of her stomach.

She flinched away from the first intrusive touch of
his tongue and Marc drew back immediately, not
wanting to hurry her into anything she wasn't ready
for. There was lots of time, he reminded himself as
he stood, all the time in the world to explore every

delightful possibility at their leisure, if not tonight then in the many nights and days yet to come.

Her mouth was sweet under his, and he kissed her for a long, unhurried while, feeling her tremble as he caressed her back and shoulders and ribs, ran his hands over her breasts, her stomach. Still holding her against him, he reached behind her and flipped the bedspread and sheets back, then gently eased her down onto the bed. She smiled up at him through the darkness, her eyes glinting with playfulness.

"I hope you were planning on joining me, Mr. d'Angelo."

Marc grinned. He pulled his shirt off impatiently, then swiftly unbuckled his leather belt. "In ways we've both only dreamed of," he assured her in a husky growl. "Should I lock the door? Your son's a pretty terrific kid, but there are some things I'd rather not have interrupted by a sudden attack of boyish curiosity."

"Maybe you'd better," Paige said with a smoky laugh. "He doesn't usually wander in during the night, but there's always a first time. I can still hear him if he calls me or has a bad dream."

Marc locked the door, then peeled off his jeans and briefs. The room was darker now, and he paused for a moment, slightly disoriented.

"Lost?" asked a softly inviting voice just beyond him.

"Completely." Two strides and he was there. Her arms came out to guide him to her, and in the next instant he was lying beside her, his arms filled with warm flesh that moved like satin against him, so pliant and alive it made him groan.

He ran his hands over her, unable to get enough of her, his mouth greedily seeking hers. She responded to his urgent kiss with a hunger as fierce as his, her tongue slippery and hot as it moved rhythmically against his. He felt a series of tiny shivers go through her, and she moaned something, her hips starting to move in the same rhythms. He slid his knee gently between hers and drew it up, feeling her thigh muscles tighten as she resisted instinctively, then loosen in that wondrous moment of trusting surrender. She was panting now, whispering his name over and over as they kissed and nuzzled, and she whimpered in anticipation as he laid his flattened palm on her stomach and gently moved it downward.

She was like silk and fire, and she gave a low, soft cry as his questing fingers found her, caressing and stroking until she was trembling and the last of her shyness melted away.

He'd never known a woman could be so responsive. Watching her through half-closed eyes, he brought her again and again to the very pinnacle, reveling in her obvious rapture until to extend the pleasure any further would have been sheer cruelty.

He eased her onto her back and slipped across her. Paige gave a sobbed whisper of encouragement, her arms locked across his back. "Yes," she urged, her breath hissing between her teeth. "Oh, Marc, yes! Now…"

"Now," he groaned in agreement.

She was so ready for him that there was only the

briefest pressure, then the magic of that first long, silken sheathing, feeling her accept the alien male strength of him unhesitatingly, enclosing him in loving warmth. At the last instant he held back, remembering how small and delicate she was and suddenly terrified of hurting her. But she gave an impatient wriggle, and he groaned aloud in gratified wonder as she arched under him, drawing him as deeply into her as their bodies would allow.

There was little need to hold back, to tease, her body and responses telling him more vividly than words that she was well beyond the need for slow preliminaries. She moaned in delighted satisfaction when he started into the long, rhythmic movements she craved. Her fingernails dug into his shoulders, her teeth were set across her lower lip as she bit back a cry, eyes tightly closed. For those last few instants, Marc knew he'd lost her momentarily to the inward, centered ecstasy that no man would ever be able to entirely share, and yet nothing could have been more satisfying than knowing he was responsible for bringing her such pleasure.

He sensed the first tiny tremors run through her, heard her intaken breath, felt her stiffen slightly under him. He went motionless, waiting until he felt her almost relax before moving again, drawing it out for her as long as he could until she arched under him, taut as a bow, and gave a long, soft cry of pleasure. When he heard her call his name, feeling every atom in her body respond so vitally to his, Marc's self-control snapped.

He was vaguely aware of Paige's long, strong legs

tightening around him, of her hands on his hips, coaxing him, of her low voice whispering things that drove
him half wild. Her mouth was under his, and he
kissed her with a savage, fierce enjoyment, losing
himself in her so completely he doubted he'd ever be
free of her again. Or ever want to be. Then everything
ceased to exist in a white-hot explosion of release so
all-encompassing he cried out her name in reckless
abandon, remembering the sleeping boy in the next
room much too late. A shudder ran through him and
he relaxed into Paige's arms, panting and deliciously
spent.

She smiled, managing to look both maidenly shy
and shamelessly satisfied at the same time, an irresistible combination that made Marc want to throw
his head back and bay at the moon in some primitive
male display of triumph.

Her smile widened impishly. "I take it, good sir,
that you are not overly disappointed that you
stayed?"

Marc chuckled contentedly. "The only thing that
disappoints me, dear lady, is the fact I didn't meet
you years ago."

"I'm glad we didn't meet years ago," Paige replied
softly. "Because you wouldn't have liked me very
much back then. I was rich and pretty and spoiled,
and not very nice at all."

"Well, you're still pretty, and I intend to do everything possible to spoil you rotten, so that just
leaves rich."

"I'm richer these days than I've ever been before,"
she whispered seriously. "Money can't buy the hap-

piness that Tyler and GingerBread Preserves have brought me. And you.''

No happier than you've made me, Marc thought as he gazed down into her face. They fitted together as perfectly as one of his father's hand-mitered joints, filling all the empty spaces in his life and making him feel complete and whole and indescribably happy. ''Just think,'' he murmured, ''if we got married, we could spend the rest of our lives like this.''

She gave a delighted laugh. ''You really will do anything to get my side of the house, won't you?''

Marc grinned. ''Your house isn't the only Mac-Kenzie structure I'm interested in, sweet lady. We could—''

The doorknob rattled noisily, cutting him off, and he felt Paige stiffen slightly. ''Mommy?''

She turned her head to look at the door. ''I'm here, honey. What is it?''

''I hafta go to the bafroom.''

Paige traded an amused glance with Marc. ''You know where it is, sweetie. Can you manage, or do you need help?''

There was a thoughtful pause. ''I can go my own self.'' Then: ''Is Marc in there wif you?''

Marc groaned softly, but Paige just smiled, her eyes holding his warmly. ''Yes, honey. He is. You go to the bathroom, then get back to bed. You'll see him in the morning, okay?''

''Okay,'' he said quite happily. ''Night, Mommy.''

''Good night, honey. Sleep tight.''

Marc stroked Paige's cheek with his thumb. ''Would you like me to leave? If I'm still here in the morning, it's going to be fairly obvious, even to a four-year-old, that I spent the night. I know he doesn't understand the implications of that yet, but it could lead to some awkward explanations. Especially if he drops the bombshell at your parents'.''

"I promised myself I'd never lie to him," she replied softly. "Or do anything I was ashamed to have him know about. Besides," she added with a giggle, "I doubt Mom would mind in the least to discover you'd spent the night. I think she was on the verge of suggesting it herself the other day."

"And your father?" Marc couldn't help asking with a grin.

Paige laughed aloud. "Fathers can't imagine their daughters sleeping with *any* man. I don't think Dad believes to this day that Peter and I shared the same bed. As far as he's concerned, Tyler's the result of immaculate conception."

Marc gave a snort of laughter, kissing the tip of her nose. Then he sobered. "I should have asked if you're…well, if you're taking something. Or—"

Paige smiled. "Marc, I'm old enough to take the responsibility. I think I'll find a father for the little boy I've got before I enlarge my family."

"Taking bids for the position?" Marc nuzzled her ear. He rolled lazily onto his side, carrying Paige with him, and drew her thigh up over his.

"Interested?"

"I could be," he assured her, not even surprised to discover he meant it. He caressed her breast until the nipple puckered, then he curled around and touched the tip of his tongue to it. His body, satisfied only minutes before, started to stir with anticipation. "I very easily could be."

Paige's breath caught very slightly. "Are we…?"

"Soon," he promised, guiding her hand. "Not yet, but very soon."

The crash was so loud that Paige sat straight up in bed before she was even fully awake, her heart pounding like a runaway locomotive. "What was *that*?"

"What was what?" muttered a sleepy voice beside her.

"Didn't you hear it? It sounded like part of the house just collapsed." Clutching the sheet to her breasts, Paige peered at the clock. "It's barely six-thirty. Who'd be making that much noise at this hour of the morning?"

"Probably just squirrels on the roof." A large warm hand started rubbing her back soothingly. "Or maybe you dreamed it. Why don't you come back down here and I'll see what I can do about getting your morning off to a better start?"

"If those were squirrels," she told him emphatically, "we are in some very serious ecological trouble!"

Her heart had started beating normally again. She let the sheet drop and turned to look down at the man stretched out beside her. Marc was lying on his back, bare to the hips, looking very rugged and big and uncompromisingly male against the delicate feminine pattern of the sheets. Deeply tanned, he looked every inch the roughneck construction worker he was these days, his chest and shoulders corded with muscle, his arms like tree limbs. His tousled hair lay in a halo on the pillow, and he smiled at her lazily, his mouth still slightly swollen from their hours of intense lovemaking, his eyes warm and gentle.

"And just what," she asked with a languorous smile, "did you have in mind?"

He reached out and stroked her bare, uptilted breast with the back of his hand, the scarred knuckles incredibly gentle. "Why don't we just make it up as we go along?"

Paige laughed softly and turned toward him, stretching out beside and across him so she could gaze down into his face. He slipped his arms around her and she kissed him lightly, then started toying almost absently with his small, hard nipples. She circled one with a fingernail, looking at him through her lashes when she heard his breath catch. "Do you like that?"

"Very much." His voice was hoarse.

"Tell me what else you like."

Marc's breathing was unsteady, and his narrowed eyes smoldered with a promising heat. He swallowed. "I like—"

His suggestion was interrupted by a horrendous crash that was even louder than the first. It came from just outside the house, and Marc started badly, swearing with fervor as he rolled clear of Paige's exploratory hand and the sheet and onto his feet. He strode to the window and pulled the drapes aside. "What the—? Uh-oh."

There was something about the way he said it that

made Paige suddenly very alert. "I don't like the sound of that 'uh-oh.'" Paige slipped out of the bed, grabbing Marc's discarded work shirt and pulling it on as she hurried to the window. As an afterthought, she picked up Marc's briefs and handed them to him. "I love the view, darling, but if Mrs. Parkdale across the street looks out and sees you standing here stark naked and in a state of such obvious—how shall I put this delicately?—arousal, she'll have a coronary." She patted him companionably on the bottom and leaned forward to look out into the street. "What's going— Oh, my God!"

"Now, don't get excited," Marc said hurriedly, balancing awkwardly on one foot as he pulled on his briefs. "It probably looks worse than it really is."

"Don't get excited? Somebody just dumped a mountain of gravel on my front lawn and backed over my car and you're telling me not to get excited?"

"He didn't really back over it. He just sort of…bumped it." Marc was struggling into his jeans.

"Mommy!" It was Tyler's voice, muffled through the door. Paige unlocked it and Tyler shot into the room, not even glancing at her as he scurried across to the window. "There was a big noise!"

"It's okay, honey," Paige told him soothingly, shooting Marc a furious glare. "I presume that gravel is yours?"

"Look at the big truck!" Tyler shouted excitedly. "Mommy, why are those men looking at our car?"

"I'll take care of it, honey." Marc paused long enough to cup Paige's face in one hand and kiss her. "Be right back."

"But—" He was out the door and down the stairs before she could finish it, and Paige gave an exasperated sigh. "That man is driving me crazy."

"What man, Mommy?" Tyler looked around curiously.

Paige smiled and walked over to give her son a hug. "How are you this morning, sweetie?"

"Fine." He hugged her back tightly, giving her an enthusiastic and decidedly sticky kiss. "I love you, Mommy!"

"I love you, too, sweetheart." She wiped a smear of peanut butter off her cheek. "You're up pretty early this morning."

"I got hungry," he said blithely.

"Uh-huh. And I don't suppose there was a squirrel out on the deck that you thought needed feeding, was there?"

"It was hungry, too."

Paige had to laugh. Then she kneeled in front of him, looking at him seriously. "Honey, I'm sorry about shouting at you yesterday. I wasn't mad at you. I was just mad at…well, at everything. But it wasn't your fault."

"That's okay, Mommy. Greg an' his daddy an' Gabriel an' me went to a Blue Jays game an' I ate two hot dogs!" He held up two chubby fingers proudly.

"Tyler…" Paige paused, then sighed, brushing his hair back from his forehead and gazing down into the brown eyes looking up at her so trustingly. "Honey, I don't know if I'm going to be able to take you to the zoo today, either. I know I told you I would, but—"

"That's okay," he repeated cheerfully. "I hafta help Marc pull some nails out of some boards today, anyway. We can go to the zoo some other time."

Paige's eyes started to sting and she hugged him fiercely. Oh, Tyler, what did I ever do to deserve you? she thought, and shut her eyes against the sudden tears, ashamed of how stoically Tyler handled all the setbacks in his young life while she seemed to fall apart every time something went wrong. There were days when he seemed more grown-up than she was.

"Ooof, Mommy!" he squeaked. "You're squashin' me!"

"Sorry, darling." Paige laughed and released him. She distastefully held up one corner of his yellow security blanket. "Do you think I could borrow this for an hour to wash it?"

"Sure." To Paige's astonishment, he dropped the blanket unconcernedly at her feet and headed for the door. "I'm gonna go down and see what's happenin'."

"Oh, no, you're not." Marc appeared at the door at that instant and scooped Tyler up under one arm. "Those trucks out there are too big, and you're too little. You're going to wash your face and brush your teeth, then you're going to get dressed and help your mother make breakfast. Then you're going to help me install the cedar wall around my hot tub. It's too big a job for one man." He winked broadly at Paige. "Then I'm going to take you and your mother to the zoo."

"Mommy can't go to the zoo," Tyler said calmly. "She hasta work."

Paige nodded regretfully. "He's right. I've decided to try to talk my bank into giving me a small-business loan, and I'm going there this morning." Marc raised a questioning eyebrow and set Tyler down. Paige shrugged. "I've got to have more operating capital, that's all there is to it. I'm in a real catch-22 situation right now. I don't have the money to buy my supplies in bulk, so I lose the quantity discounts, which means I'm spending more money than I need to, which in turn means—"

"—you don't have the capital to buy in bulk," Marc finished for her. "I was wondering why you made up such small batches of everything."

"Because I never have enough jars or supplies. I have to get the money from one customer to buy enough supplies to make up the order for my next customer. It's like juggling eggs while on roller skates. One wrong move and I've got an omelet!"

"Sounds risky. Get sick and lose a day—or spend a day at the zoo—and the whole thing could come down like a house of cards."

"Exactly," said Paige glumly. Then she smiled at him. "Enough of that. Do you like blueberry pancakes?"

Marc groaned. "Lady, you have discovered the way to my heart." He grinned mischievously, his eyes holding hers. "One or two ways to my heart, come to think of it." Then he added in an undertone, "I suppose the possibility we might manage to slip away for a couple of hours this afternoon to discover some more is too much to hope for?"

Paige's heart did a little somersault at the husky

promise in his voice. "As a matter of fact, a little boy I know has pre-kindergarten from noon to two."

Marc slipped his arms around her waist and nuzzled her ear. "Meet me up here at twelve sharp," he purred. "I'm going to take that whole two hours to make it so good for you that you'll figure last night was just a warm-up." He nipped her earlobe, and Paige had to fight to catch her breath. "And we won't have to worry about anyone hearing us."

Paige blushed when she thought of last night. "I can't remember ever being like that before," she whispered in embarrassment.

"I love it," Marc growled. He slipped his hands up under the shirt and started caressing her bottom, lifting and pressing her against him. "It's the most erotic thing in the world, watching you, listening to those little catches in your voice when you're whispering my name, the way you give that little startled moan when I—"

"Marc!" Paige sagged against him. "For heaven's sake, if you don't stop it…"

He chuckled throatily against her ear. "Twelve o'clock, sweetheart. Can you wait?"

"I don't know," she whispered quite truthfully, already aching with want. "I'm liable to make a shambles out of that meeting with my banker this morning."

"You should be relaxed and calm for that," he whispered considerately. "I'll run down and fix Tyler's breakfast, then meet you in the shower in ten minutes. It'll be quick, but I can guarantee it'll be good."

"Oh, Marc, don't tempt me," Paige whispered. "I'd love to, but…" She glanced wordlessly at Tyler who was staring avidly out the bedroom window.

"I suppose it would be wishful thinking to hope breakfast might keep him occupied," Marc agreed with a groaning laugh. "Besides, there are some things I don't like to rush."

"Such as?"

"Such as…" Marc kissed her ear, then whispered something so deliciously explicit that Paige's breath caught. She giggled, blushing furiously, and Tyler, curious, glanced around. "Getting hungry, short stuff?" Marc asked smoothly, letting his arms slip regretfully from around Paige. He gave her a broad smile, then took Tyler's outstretched hand and strolled toward the door.

"Mommy, are you coming for breakfast?"

"I'll be right down, honey," Paige assured her son, her voice slightly unsteady. "Right after I have a shower."

"Solo?" Marc paused at the top of the stairs and looked at her, his eyes dancing with mischief.

"Solo," Paige replied with a low laugh.

"What's a solo?" Tyler asked brightly as he started down the stairs.

"Solo means being alone," Marc told him. His eyes, serious now, held Paige's. "It's one of those things every man thinks he wants more of—until the day he meets a very special person and realizes that solo's not the best way at all."

And Paige, still aglow with the touch and taste of him, smiled, filled with the growing awareness of just how important to her this tall, blue-eyed man was becoming.

"Marc, I could kill you for this." Paige gazed at her car in resigned despair. The truck that had delivered the gravel now sitting in the middle of her front lawn had backed into it somehow, caving in both doors on the driver's side. Bare metal gleamed through the scrapes.

Marc's arm tightened around her waist in a sympathetic hug. "Sorry, sweetheart. Petros was supposed to deliver it tomorrow. And he was supposed to dump it in the backyard." He reached out and tried to straighten the outside mirror on the Volvo. It came off in his hand and he looked at it, startled. "I'll get T.K. to haul it over to the body shop and knock the dents out of it."

"I should get him to haul it out to the wrecker and put it out of its misery," Paige admitted. "The poor old thing's just about done for. It'll cost more to repair than it would to buy a new one."

"It's got a couple of years under its hood yet," Marc assured her. He eased his fingers into the front pocket of his tight blue jeans and extracted a set of car keys, then dangled them in front of Paige. "In the meantime, drive the 911."

"Your Porsche?" Paige's voice lifted in astonishment and she turned to look at the sleek sports car parked at the curb. Its brilliant red finish gleamed like glass. "Are you kidding? I'm scared to even walk by it in case I scratch it."

Marc turned her hand palm upward, then dropped

the keys into it and folded her fingers over them one at a time. "It's yours. At least until the Volvo's running. I use the truck all the time anyway." He nodded toward the battered green pickup parked behind the Porsche.

"Marc…"

"Shut up, Paige," he told her calmly, grinning down at her. "Do as I say, or I'll be forced to take drastic measures."

"Such as?"

"Such as dragging you upstairs and making love to you until you beg me to stop."

"Has anyone ever told you that you've got an obsessive personality?" Paige asked with a laugh. "Last night I'm sure we—"

"—only whetted my appetite," he finished with a salacious grin. "Remember we have a date upstairs at twelve. Give your banker my regards, and tell him you can't stay past eleven-thirty because you've got an insatiable naked man waiting in bed for you."

"I'll tell him," Paige promised dryly, turning her face up happily for his lingering kiss. "Your dad and Greg just drove up. Are you going to hear the end of this?"

"My dad's dream in life is to see me married and settled down, and Greg's already convinced we have something going." He emphasized his lack of concern by kissing her again, more thoroughly this time. "And that was for Mrs. Parkdale. She's been watching us from the kitchen window."

Paige smiled against his mouth. "I'll see you at twelve. Sharp." Then, straightening her pale yellow suit jacket and adjusting the small veiled hat to a jaunty angle, she looked around for Tyler. He was happily investigating the gravel pile, and Paige groaned and hurried to rescue him before he got his pants and jacket any dirtier. "Are you sure you don't mind keeping an eye on Tyler while I'm gone? I can still drop him off at the baby-sitter's."

Patiently, Marc turned her toward the Porsche and gave her a gentle push. "Go. And watch the clutch the first few times you let it out. It's got practically no play, and by the time you realize you're in gear you can be halfway down the block."

"Don't forget that the playschool bus comes by about a quarter to twelve and—" Paige stopped, seeing the expression on Marc's face. "I'm going," she said meekly. "Wish me luck."

"You've got it, sweet stuff. Give 'em hell."

"Yeah," Paige murmured to herself as she slid cautiously into the Porsche. I don't have any choice.

The curved driver's seat fit her like a glove, and Paige looked appreciatively around the luxuriously appointed interior of the car. It smelled of expensive leather and Marc's cologne, a solid masculine combination she found oddly comforting, and she smiled as she put the key in the ignition and turned it. I'll do it, she told herself confidently. I'm not coming back from that bank without the money!

Nine

"**I** just know I didn't get it." Paige paced the dining room restlessly, her high heels clicking on the hardwood floor. She paused to stare out into the yard, arms clasped tightly under her breasts. "They're not going to approve it."

Marc watched her for a moment or two, then pushed himself away from the doorjamb where he'd been leaning and went over to stand behind her. He wrapped his arms around her and rested his chin on top of her head, watching a big gray squirrel burying something in the lawn. Bits of grass and dirt flew as it dug furiously. "You don't know that, honey. Getting approval on a loan like that is just routine."

The squirrel tucked its treasure into the hole and started to cover it, patting the dirt down with its front paws. Paige shook her head and stepped out of his embrace, pacing again. "No, that's not it. He was frowning, Marc."

"Bankers always frown. They're paid to frown. It reassures the customers that their money's being handled by people who take the job seriously."

But she didn't smile. "They're not going to give it to me. They think I'm being frivolous. That I don't know what I'm doing."

"What did you tell him you wanted the money for?"

"I already told you. I explained that I'm scrambling now trying to get ahead of my orders, that with extra jars and labels and other supplies, I can get a bit ahead and then branch out and—what's wrong?"

"Paige—" He looked at her, then shook his head, wishing he'd kept his mouth shut. The expression on her face boded no good, but he was in over his head now with nowhere to go but straight ahead. "I can't tell you how to run your business, honey. I don't know a thing about it, but from where I'm standing, you seem to be scattered. Unfocused. You can't seem to make up your mind if you're selling ginger marmalade or barbecue spice or spaghetti sauce or half a dozen other things. They're all good products, but the market's different for each. It seems to me you're going in too many directions at once, that's all. At least until you get firmly established."

"You're right," Paige said in a clipped voice. "You can't tell me how to run my business. Stick to your hammers and nails, and leave the gourmet food business to me."

Marc flushed. It was his own fault for getting into

this in the first place. She was as touchy as a cat in heat about anything to do with GingerBread, and if he had a brain in his head he'd leave it right there.

As though knowing what he was thinking, Paige suddenly walked over to him and slipped her arms around him, tucking her head under his chin. "I'm sorry, Marc," she whispered.

Marc massaged her back and shoulders with both hands. He ached with frustration, wishing he could ease her worry. "It'll be all right," he murmured, unable to shake off the sense that he was lying. He took off her hat and set it on the table, then started unpinning her hair. It spilled around his hands like sun-warmed water, and he buried his face in it, his arms tightening around her. "Tyler won't be home for another hour. Come upstairs and let me make you forget all about this for a little while."

But she shook her head and pushed away from him, frowning. "I'm just not in the mood right now, Marc. I keep going over everything I said today, trying to figure out where I went wrong."

Marc had his mouth half open to tell her that he was certain he could get her into the mood and that an hour's lovemaking was exactly what she needed to put the banker out of her mind. Then he thought better of it, not sure his motives were as altruistic as he'd like to think. The truth was that after spending last night with this woman, after making love with her with an intensity and caring that had shaken him to the core, he was finding it difficult to think of much else.

His body was already responding to the scent and

touch of her, and he gritted his teeth and forced himself to keep from kissing her soundly. "I should get back to work. Pop and Greg are giving me a hand putting down the carpet in the master bedroom, and they'll be wondering where I am." She nodded absently and he paused, watching her, wishing he could say something to make her feel better. Damn that banker, he thought savagely. All he'd looked at were cold facts and figures. None of his charts took in caring or pride or the kind of single-minded obstinacy that could take a losing operation and turn it around simply by the sheer power of will.

Paige didn't even hear Marc leave. She turned around to ask him if he wanted a cup of coffee and discovered that he wasn't there. She let her shoulders slump with weariness as she walked slowly through the house. As she started up the stairs she noticed that the Navaho blanket had been draped to one side, giving easy access to the hole in the wall. She smiled to herself as she walked up to the bedroom and started to change. The room was still filled with Marc's musky male scent, and she looked around at the clothing still scattered across the floor, the unmade bed. The memory of the two of them in here scant hours ago, naked bodies intimately locked, filled her mind. It took no effort at all to imagine being here with him again. Even the mere thought of his touch made her skin tingle, and she gave her head an impatient shake to dispel the image.

She didn't have time for that right now. She had to figure out what she was going to do if the bank turned her down. Unwillingly, she thought of her fa-

ther. He'd love to help her. There'd be strings, of
course. He'd want her to move back home; he'd want
to see Tyler more often; he'd feel no compunction
about advising her how to spend "his" money. In
spite of all that, temptation flickered through Paige.
Then it died, and she took a deep breath and eased it
out again almost regretfully. Sorry, Daddy, she told
him silently. If I turn to you for help this once, then
it'll just be easier next time. I *have* to do this on my
own.

She found herself smiling in spite of the fear nibbling away at the edges of her mind. There was one
thing her father had given her that she wouldn't have
gotten this far without: the Pricefield stubborn streak.
"Thanks, Daddy," she said aloud, smiling at her reflection in the mirror. It was there, she knew: the same
firm set to the chin, the no-nonsense glint to the
brown eyes. She was Harrington J. Pricefield's daughter, no doubt about it. "You're going to be proud of
me," she told him firmly.

The next three days, spent waiting to hear from the
bank, were the longest of Paige's life. Every time the
phone rang she jumped like a startled cat, crossing
her fingers as she reached for the receiver. And every
time it was someone other than Frank Hollingsworth
of the loans department, she fell into gloomy despair.

But in another way, Paige had to admit, they were
also three of the happiest days of her life. Marc made
sure of that. He didn't intrude in either her life or her
work, yet he always seemed to be there, comforting
her when she needed it, making her laugh when she

felt like crying, filling her hours with a soul-deep contentment she'd never known before. He'd pop through the rabbit hole at odd hours of the day to share a companionable cup of coffee with her, to bring in her mail or play handyman when something fell apart. Sometimes he'd be busy on his own side of the house and she wouldn't see him for hours, then she'd look around and find him standing leaning against the doorjamb, watching her with that warm, loving smile that made her melt.

He was always bringing her little gifts: flowers, a sample of his mother's incredible Italian baking, strange imported cheese from the local deli. And once it was an entire gallon of Häagen-Dasz Vanilla Swiss Almond ice cream. They'd sat out on the deck with Tyler, and the three of them had eaten it right out of the container with long-handled spoons, Bub getting his share in a saucer.

Paige was surprised to discover that Marc was an excellent cook. Every evening he'd invite her and Tyler over to his side of the house for Chinese, Middle Eastern or Mexican food. Dishes washed, they'd sit on the floor in front of a crackling fire with brandy or wine and talk quietly while Tyler and Bub played. Then later, when child and cat were asleep, he'd lead her upstairs and they'd spend hours making love, falling asleep in each other's arms to waken before dawn and make love again, slowly and tenderly. And it was sometime during those three days that Paige realized she'd fallen in love.

"…ice-cream cone?"

Paige blinked, suddenly realizing that Marc was

speaking to her. "Pardon?"

He laughed softly, wrapping his arm around her shoulders and pulling her against him as they strolled lazily down one of the narrow side streets not far from Chestnut Manor. Tyler was half a block ahead of them, talking earnestly with a small Yorkshire terrier tied to a decorative wrought-iron lamp post in front of the ice cream store. "I was just wondering if I could sweet-talk you into sharing an ice-cream cone with me."

"If it's pistachio."

"Pistachio it is. Tyler!" The boy's head shot up, glowing like gold in the early-evening sun. "What flavor, sport?"

"'Stachio!"

"Looks like it's unanimous." Marc kissed the top of Paige's head.

She smiled as she watched him disappear into the mass of people in the little store and strolled over to join Tyler by the lamp post. Half restaurant and half ice cream parlor, it was a favorite social gathering place for the neighborhood. Most of the people strolling around, licking ice-cream cones, were young and well-dressed, part of the generation that had moved in a few years ago, buying up the old Victorian row houses and mansions and renovating them.

Paige loved this part of Toronto. It didn't have the dignified elegance of Rosedale, but it had a friendly, small-town feel and community spirit to it that made her forget she was living in the center of Canada's largest city. It had once been home to predominantly

Irish blue-collar workers who had made up Toronto's work force a century ago and whose food staple had given the area its name. Cabbagetown was now a delightfully eclectic mix of millionaires and down-and-outs, of century-old Georgian mansions and tiny Victorian cottages and narrow row houses. Huge maple and chestnut trees canopied streets lined with tiny expensive restaurants, shops filled with designer clothes, health clubs, salad bars, delis, specialty food stores and fruit markets that overflowed onto the sidewalks every morning with baskets of vegetables and freshly cut flowers. All of which, Paige found herself musing, were perfect markets for GingerBread Preserves.

She caught the direction of her thoughts and smiled, putting them firmly out of her mind. She'd promised herself that she wouldn't think of GingerBread Preserves or the bank until they got back to the house.

Marc came out of the tiny store just then, carrying two double-scoop cones. Tyler came racing over and took his carefully, then Marc slipped his free arm around Paige's shoulders and they strolled across the street and into the small park.

"First taste." He held the cone out and Paige licked the ice cream, laughing as he bent down to share it with her. "Come on, let's sit down."

He nodded toward an old-fashioned wooden bench under a chestnut tree. They sat down and Paige leaned back with a sigh, gazing around happily at the other after-dinner strollers out enjoying the warm evening. The air was lightly perfumed with barnyard smells from the petting farm just behind them, and she could hear a cow lowing somewhere.

"Glad I talked you into taking some time off?"

Paige nodded. "You may wish I hadn't when I'm up until two this morning bottling the last of that peach jam."

"I'll give you a hand." Marc swirled his tongue around the cone expertly, then handed it back to her. "I have something for you, by the way. Frank Hollingsworth down at the bank gave it to me when I was there paying the phone bill."

At the banker's name, Paige's stomach fluttered. She handed the cone back to Marc untouched and stared at the envelope he'd taken out of his shirt pocket and was holding toward her. "They've turned me down," she said, hands clenched in her lap. "I told you they would."

"Will you open the damned thing?" Marc told her impatiently.

Paige reached out and took the envelope unwillingly. She opened it even more reluctantly and drew out the single sheet of paper, unfolded it and stared down at the few neatly typed sentences. So sure was she that they were turning down her request for the loan, she had to read the letter twice before she realized what it said. "I don't believe it," she whispered, her eyes widening.

"What?" Marc looked at her, ice cream poised. "Paige?"

"It—" She looked up at him. "They've approved the loan." Slowly, as the reality of what had just happened filtered through her daze, she started to smile and she flung her arms around Marc's neck and kissed him soundly. "Oh, Marc, they're giving me the money!"

"They're not complete fools," he murmured, kissing her back just as soundly. "Congratulations, Mrs. MacKenzie. You've done it again."

"I really did, didn't I?" she asked in amazement, sitting back and staring at the letter in her hand. "Holy cow, do you know what this means? I can buy those pretty new jars I was looking at last week and get new labels printed and—" She stopped and looked at him suspiciously. "You knew, didn't you?"

Marc laughed quietly. He reached across and dabbed ice cream on the end of her nose. "Not exactly, but Hollingsworth was smiling when he handed it to me, so I figured it was good news."

"And you kept me in suspense all this time?"

"I figured it was worth a small celebration." He held up the ice-cream cone, smiling at her lazily. "There's a bottle of champagne on ice back at the house. And something else."

Paige laughed delightedly. "What could be better than pistachio ice cream and champagne?"

"This." He took something else out of his shirt pocket and held it out to her.

Paige stared at the small blue velvet box, then, slowly, she looked up and met his eyes. "Marc?"

He smiled gently. "Open it."

She watched her own hand go out to the box as though in a dream, watched her unsteady fingers lift the lid. "Oh…Marc." There were four diamonds, set in a curved S-pattern, flanking a large square-cut emerald. She swallowed, hardly daring to believe this was happening.

"I was going to do it properly, with the champagne and the kneeling routine and everything, but I couldn't wait any longer." He reached out and put a finger under her chin, lifting her face so she was looking at him. "Marry me, Paige MacKenzie?"

"Oh, Marc!" She gave a gulp, half laughing and half in tears. "You weren't kidding when you said you'd do anything to get my side of Chestnut Manor, were you?"

He gave a chuckle. "And you didn't believe me, did you?"

"But it—it's so sudden. I mean, we've never talked about getting married or...or anything like that."

"Not in so many words, I guess." His eyes caressed her face, filled with wonder. "But I love you, Paige. I'm sure you must know that by now. And if I weren't sure you felt the same way, I wouldn't have bought this." Gently, he took the ring from its velvet case and slipped it onto her left hand. "I know you wouldn't marry me or anybody else until you got your business up and running. But when Hollingsworth gave me that letter today, I knew there was no reason for us to wait."

"I—" Paige's voice cracked and she closed her eyes. "Oh, damn! Can we go home?" He looked so stricken that Paige had to laugh. "It's just that I think I'm going to start crying in a minute, and I don't want to embarrass us in public."

A look of relief washed over Marc's face. "Is this your way of saying yes?"

In spite of the tears that threatened to overwhelm her momentarily, Paige burst into laughter and slipped her arms around his neck again, burying her face in his shoulder. "Yes, I guess it is."

Marc hugged her, kissing the top of her head. "You haven't said you love me yet, you know. I think there's some law that says when a man asks a woman to marry him, she's supposed to tell him she loves him."

"Of course I love you, you idiot," Paige sobbed against his neck. "If I didn't love you, do you think I'd be bawling all over your shirt collar right now?"

"Romantic little devil, aren't you?" Marc cradled her against him, rubbing her shoulders.

"Oh, Marc!" As always, he made her laugh. Dabbing at her nose and trying to blink her eyes clear, Paige lifted her head. "I think I wilted your collar."

"To hell with my collar. Let's go home."

"Mommy, are you laughin' or cryin'?" Tyler clambered up onto the bench beside her, staring up at Paige worriedly.

"Both," Paige told him with a sob of laughter, hugging him fiercely. He gave a squeak of protest and she released him finally, noticing the empty cone in his hand. "What happened to your ice cream?"

"It falled off, and a big dog ate it," he remarked sadly.

"Oh, no!" Still laughing, Paige shook her head slowly and brushed the hair off Tyler's forehead. "You poor little guy. You really have a hard time some days, don't you?"

"Here." Trying to contain his own laughter, Marc

reached past her and handed Tyler the other cone. "I always carry a spare."

Tyler's face brightened. He took the cone and started licking it happily, Paige's tears and the thieving dog forgotten.

Paige looked over her shoulder at Marc, smiling. "Sure you're ready for this instant-family stuff, d'Angelo? A few weeks of this, and you may wish you'd stayed single."

He slipped his arms around her waist and pulled her back against him, kissing the side of her throat. "The day I sold my contracting company and started helping Pop at Angel Construction, I knew I'd done the right thing. The day I walked into Chestnut Manor, I knew I wanted it. And the instant I set eyes on you, I knew the same thing. It's as though the four of you—Angel, the house, you, Tyler—have all been waiting to converge at this exact point in my life when I'm finally ready for you." He gave her an extra hug, then took her hand and tugged her to her feet. "Now let's go home, break open that champagne and celebrate this properly."

"Who needs champagne?" Paige asked happily as she nestled into the curve of his arm. They started strolling back toward Chestnut Manor, Tyler padding along contentedly beside them. "I'm giddy already."

The screwdriver slipped, digging a gouge out of Marc's left thumb and an even deeper one in the freshly plastered bathroom wall just above where he was mounting the towel rack. He swore with feeling, then glanced down at Tyler, who was sitting on the edge of the bathtub, watching with wide-eyed interest.

"That's another one of those words you don't say around your mother," he advised the boy calmly.

"Okay," Tyler said agreeably. "Do you want a Band-Aid?"

Marc chuckled. "It's okay, Tyler, thanks." He tossed the towel bar and screwdriver onto the vanity and wiped his hands on his jeans, leaving a bloody smear. "Let's call it a day, sport. I need a bottle of beer. How about you?"

"Yeah!" Tyler skipped along beside him. "And a cookie."

Bub appeared from nowhere to pad along beside them, tail wafting gently in the air. As they started down the curving sweep of stairs to the living room, Tyler reached up and took Marc's hand. Bub bounded past them and disappeared.

Marc looked down at Tyler. "Where's your blanket?"

"Dunno." Tyler shrugged, unconcerned.

Marc smiled to himself. Paige had mentioned last night that Tyler had finally eased his dependency on the ratty old blanket. She always kept it handy for the occasional setback, usually when he was tired or cranky, but he'd go for days without even thinking about it now.

Too bad I can't give up my dependency on cigarettes as painlessly, Marc thought glumly, wishing he had one right now. Last-minute bachelor nerves? he found himself wondering. He and Paige had sat up half the night, celebrating their engagement with the chilled champagne as he'd promised, talking and laughing and making plans. Sometime during that long night they'd made love for hours, sharing something so special, so profound, that it had left her weeping in his arms and him so shaken he'd lain awake until nearly dawn.

He took a deep breath and flexed his shoulders, trying to ease the knot of tension across them. No doubts. Not about Paige, anyway. But whenever he thought of the slightly underhanded way he'd arranged the entire thing, he felt a little twinge of apprehensive guilt. He frowned as he pulled the fridge open and took out a bottle of beer and the carton of milk. Still frowning, he poured the milk into a glass and set it on the table in front of Tyler, then bent over and put a generous splash into Bub's bowl. He pried the cap off the beer and took a long swallow of it, leaning back against the counter and crossing his legs. Sooner or later he was going to have to tell her, he supposed. Preferably about ten years from now, he brooded, after the money had been paid back, the loan forgotten. Maybe by then she'd be ready to forgive him.

"Are you and Mommy getting married?" Tyler asked suddenly. He dipped the peanut butter cookie into his glass of milk.

Marc looked at the boy in surprise, then gave a snort of laughter. "Sure are, half-pint. Do you approve?"

"Yep." Tyler chewed reflectively. "Does that mean you're gonna be my daddy from now on?"

"That's exactly what it means. It also means that

Greg, Roman, Vic and Gabe are your uncles, Angelica and Maria are your aunts—you haven't met them yet—and that Uncle Vincenzo is really your new grandfather.'' Tyler looked a little dazed at all this, and Marc laughed. ''Don't worry about it. You'll get it all straightened out in time.''

''If you're my daddy, then is Bub my kitty, too?''

So much for priorities, Marc thought with a wry grin. ''Yes, Bub is your kitty, too.''

That seemed to satisfy him. He nodded and turned his attention to a second peanut butter cookie, leaving Marc to his brooding thoughts.

It was nearly an hour later that Marc heard the Porsche pull into the driveway. He was flat on his back on his kitchen floor with his head and shoulders squeezed into the narrow cupboard under the sink, and he glanced at his wristwatch with a frown. She'd gone over to the bank to sign those papers three hours ago. It shouldn't have taken her this long.

He stared up at the threaded coupling above his head, then shook his head impatiently. Quit worrying about it, he told himself. There was no way she could have found out. Those bank records were confidential. But in spite of his reassurance, his stomach gave a guilty little twist. He swore unimaginatively and picked up the wrench again, attacking the balky fitting.

Footsteps crossed the unfinished kitchen floor, crisp and sharp. Paige's high heels. They stopped beside his right foot and Marc grinned. ''Hi.''

There was no answer. He finished threading the pipe together, then gingerly eased himself out from under the sink, wincing as he hit his elbow on the edge of the cupboard. Hot and tousled, he looked up at her. And felt chilled when those russet eyes, as cool as smoked glass, met his. Trying to act very unconcerned, he got to his feet, brushing sawdust off his jeans. "What's up?"

"Nothing very important," she said tersely. She held up a folded document, then tossed it onto the counter. "That's yours, by the way. One of the tellers at the bank asked me to give it to you."

Warily, Marc reached for it. He had a sinking feeling he knew what it was, but he unfolded it and perused it.

"She asked me to remind you that it needs your signature. As guarantor of the loan."

"Paige..."

"Damn you, how could you do this to me?" she demanded, all pretense at calmness gone. A spot of red blazed high on each cheekbone, and her eyes glowed with anger. "I never had a chance, did I? They weren't even going to give me the time of day until you phoned and offered to make the loan yourself."

Marc tossed the loan agreement down and raked his fingers through his hair. "I called after you came back that afternoon. Just to give my name as a reference, hoping it would swing the vote your way. But they told me it wasn't enough. That the head branch didn't like handling risky, small-business loans."

"So you figured you'd just 'help out' by lending me the money yourself. Incognito, of course." She stared at him, very pale but for the scarlet on her cheeks. "I don't know why I'm so surprised. You've been 'helping out' ever since you moved in here, taking over my life, making yourself indispensable."

Marc didn't say anything, knowing now that the whim that had made him call the bank was one of the biggest mistakes of his life. "Paige, I'm sorry," he finally said wearily. "I just wanted to—"

"Help." Her lip curled over the word, its taste obviously unpalatable. "Well, no thanks, Mr. d'Angelo. I can manage very well on my own."

She held up a small blue velvet box and Marc felt something wrench inside him. It was only then that he realized the third finger on her left hand was bare. "Paige! Honey—"

"I won't marry a man who sneaks around behind my back and lies to me, Marc." She put the box on the counter, then tossed the car keys beside it. "And thanks for the use of the Porsche. But I think I'll make my own way from now on." Then she turned away and walked out the door.

"Hey…! *Hey!*"

Paige ignored Marc's angry shout, too angry herself to want to think about anything except getting over to her own side of Chestnut Manor. Why couldn't he have just kept out of it?

"Damn it, where do you think you're going?" Marc strode by her and planted himself solidly in front of the hole in his wall, hands on hips, mouth and chin hard.

"Get out of my way," Paige said impatiently, trying to go around him.

But Marc deftly blocked her escape. "You're not

leaving here until we talk this out. You don't walk in here and drop a bombshell like this on me without some sort of explanation.''

''Explanation?'' Paige stared at him, hands on her own hips now in an unconscious parody of his defiant stance. ''If you can't understand what you've done—how important it is for me to do this on my own, without charity, without help—then all the explanations in the world aren't going to help.''

''And this?'' he nearly bellowed, holding up the ring box. ''You love me, for God's sake! You don't just hand a man his ring back because he made an error in judgment and you're a little hot under the collar.''

''I'm not a little hot under the collar,'' she explained with exaggerated pleasantness. ''And you did not make an error in judgment—you just invalidated everything I've worked three years for.''

Marc stared at her. ''What in the name of heaven are you talking about?''

''I've fought tooth and nail to make it this far on my own, without asking for help from anyone,'' Paige's voice was shaking, and she knew her cheeks were flushed with anger. She couldn't remember the last time she'd been so mad at anyone, and the fact he just stood there demanding answers, pretending he didn't know what she was talking about, was making her madder by the passing second. ''Why should I turn down every offer of help my father's made, only to turn around and accept it from you? I don't want to be indebted to you any more than to him. Or to anyone else. I'm doing this on my own, Marc. So butt out of my life!''

''I don't believe this!'' Marc wheeled away from her, clenched fists raised as though he'd like to punch them both through the wall. He settled for snarling a pungent four-letter oath instead, striking the wall once, hard, with his open palms for emphasis. Then he turned back to face her, breathing heavily. ''You are without a doubt the most stubborn, hardheaded woman I've ever met! You're like a drug addict with this obsession of your. You're so fixated on the target that you can't see anything or anyone else.''

''I can see perfectly clearly that you're trying to play Mr. Fix-It with my life the same way you've been playing it with my house,'' Paige shot back. ''If one of us is obsessed with something, it's you. You can't stand the thought that there might be something going on that you haven't meddled in yet.''

''Meddled? You call trying to help the woman I love meddling?''

''Yes, I call it meddling. You're just like my father! The two of you are 'fixers.' You're never happy unless something's broken so you can take charge and be all heroic and manly. Well, forget it. That's just another form of manipulation, Marc. Another way men like you and Daddy tie your women to you.''

He stared down at her with an almost helpless frustration. ''What the hell is it you want from us, Paige?''

''Nothing!'' It was a cry of anguish, and Paige felt all the anger and frustration of the past twenty-seven years burst through her. "I don't want anything from you. Can't you understand that? I'm just trying to grow up!"

"Then do it."

Ten

The three words were clipped. They fell into the sudden silence that followed her outburst like stones into a pond, sending ripples through the room. Paige blinked at him.

Marc eased his breath out between his teeth, scrubbing his hand through his hair. "I'm not trying to run your life for you, Paige," he said gently. "I'm just trying to give you a helping hand. As a friend. As a lover. It doesn't mean I'm interfering. It just means I love you."

"That's what Daddy says, too."

He seemed to have expended all his fierce anger, and he was looking down at her very calmly now. "You don't have to be afraid of love, Paige. Loving me isn't admitting weakness. It doesn't mean one of us has to be vulnerable to the other."

"I know that," she replied testily. "I'm not afraid of falling in love. That's not what this is all about."

"I'm starting to think that's exactly what it's about." He stared at her for a long while. "Was I too easy? Is that why you won't marry me—because I fell in love with you without a fight? Do you figure that if something's easy, it can't be any good?"

"Of course not! Quit trying to change the topic."

"Then why are you making it so hard for yourself, Paige?" he asked wearily. "Do you figure that if you make it twice as hard it means you're twice as good? Twice as deserving?"

"What are you talking about?" she burst out impatiently. "I came in here to tell you to stop trying to run my life, and now you're doing some deep psychological profile on me, trying to prove I'm crazy for wanting to succeed."

"You're not crazy for wanting to succeed, Paige. What's a little crazy is the way you're going about it. You go out of your way to make it hard on yourself. Sometimes I wonder if you're not really secretly trying to fail."

"Fail?" Paige's voice rose on the word.

"It's not easy, doing what you're doing—starting a business, buying this house, raising Tyler. But it's pretty scary, too. If you fail, then there's no more reason not to call it quits and go home. Where it's nice and safe and—"

"I'm not going to fail." The words were cold steel.

"No?" One dark eyebrow lifted slowly. "You've been trying your damnedest so far, sweetheart. You've turned GingerBread Preserves into an octopus, branching out into so many directions I doubt even you know how many products you're trying to sell. Common sense says pick a few things and perfect them, but that would be too easy.'' He drawled the word sarcastically. ''Now, of course, it's academic. Without that loan, you're going to go under by the end of the month. You admitted it yourself.'' He smiled amiably and shrugged his shoulder toward the wall behind him. ''In another month or so, I figure Chestnut Manor will be all mine.''

''Like hell it will! I won't give that house up even if it means selling my jam on street corners. I have a good product, and I can make GingerBread Preserves one of the best little homegrown businesses this city's ever seen.''

''Then do it!'' His snapping blue eyes challenged hers. ''If you really think you're so good, hotshot, put your jam where you mouth is and prove it. There's five grand sitting in the bank waiting for you.'' He pulled the folded loan application from his shirt pocket and waved it in front of her like a matador flipping scarlet at a bull. ''You think you can do it? Then get out there and prove you've got what it takes. And stop acting like that spoiled little Rosedale brat you've been trying to outgrow.''

''All right, I will! You just watch me!'' So furious she was almost seeing double, Paige didn't even realize what he was up to until it was too late. She stood there, mouth open, staring at him as it gradually dawned on her that he had just neatly tricked her into doing exactly what he'd wanted her to do in the first place: accept that loan. ''I...you...'' she sputtered helplessly, floundering around for some dignified retreat. But there wasn't any. He'd snapped the trap closed behind her and simply stood there now smiling beatifically, as though completely innocent of any double-dealing.

"I'll sign this and drop it off at the bank tomorrow morning." Marc held up the loan agreement, then folded it and tucked it into his shirt pocket, his eyes never leaving hers. Then he tossed the keys for the Porsche at her, taking her so by surprise that she caught them before she realized what they were. "If you're going to do some shopping today, you'll need wheels." Then he turned and walked back into the kitchen.

Paige sighed. Some of her indignant anger had dissipated, leaving her feeling curiously empty. She slipped through the hole in Marc's wall into her side of the house, bringing the blanket down over it with a sharp tug. That damned wall was becoming a symbol of everything that was wrong with her life. Like it, her resolve was crumbling away a bit at a time, the mortar of willpower holding it together riddled with doubt. And it was about as impervious to intruders as this wall was: Marc wandered in and out of her life as easily as he did her house, making himself equally at home in both. Just how high was she going to have to build it, she wondered, to keep him on the other side?

And the money? She sat down on the carpeted steps and planted her chin in her palms, staring across the living room. Quite honestly, she didn't know. It would be there for her if she wanted it. Enough to make her dream come true. But nothing came without a price tag. And just what, she found herself thinking, would she wind up paying for Marc's generosity? Just her heart? Or her very independence?

Marc swore and rolled onto his back, glaring at the glowing dial on the digital clock by his bed. Two-thirty. Ten minutes since he'd last checked. He rubbed his eyes with the back of his arm, wondering if Paige was having half as much trouble sleeping tonight as he was. He'd bought this king-size bed when he'd moved in here because he hated feeling confined, but tonight he felt lost in it. Emptiness spread out on either side of him, emphasizing his solitude.

He missed her, damn it. He missed the sound of her soft breathing beside him in the darkness, the feel of her firm little bottom tucked against him, the way he'd wake up in the morning and find her legs all tangled up with his. He glowered up at the ceiling. Who'd have thought it possible? he wondered miserably. He'd always relished his single life, and here he was tossing and turning half the night because he missed Paige's warm presence beside him.

He swore again, throwing his arm over his eyes as if to shut out the memory of the anger on her face when she'd faced him that afternoon. What a mess he'd made of that! And yet for the life of him, he couldn't figure out what he'd done that was so unforgivably bad. What did she expect from him, anyway? Damn it, he loved her! And loving meant helping…didn't it?

He rolled onto his side with a growl, punching the pillow into a ball. Where did helping end, and interfering start? He could remember a couple of times when he'd been growing up that Roman or Gabriel had confused one for the other, seeing it as part of the role as older brother to "help," whether help had been requested or not. Even now, thinking back to that day in grade seven when he'd carelessly told Gabe about his dream of taking Karin Delgrado to the school dance, he still winced. Gabe, wanting to help his kid brother, had "arranged things." Marc could still recall the mortification he'd suffered when the "arrangement" became public knowledge and the entire world had discovered that Marc d'Angelo was too chicken to ask a girl out without his brother's help.

Marc groaned aloud and rolled onto his back again, kicking the sheet off. He sat up and swung his legs over the side of the bed, then sat there, elbows on knees, head in hands. Maybe she was right. Maybe in his well-intentioned effort to help her, he'd taken away her options like Gabriel had taken away his with Karin Delgrado. He got to his feet and paced the darkness restlessly. He paused by the dresser for a moment, then pulled open the top drawer and took out the one package of cigarettes he hadn't thrown out. He removed a cigarette, then lit it and dragged in a deep lungful of smoke in relief and satisfaction.

He'd just done it for her, damn it! It drove him crazy watching her working those endless eighteen-hour days, ignoring her own needs and those of her son, driving herself into exhaustion as she chased the right dream for the wrong reason. He'd been there, too. And he'd just been trying to keep her from making the same mistakes.

Marc looked at the cigarette, then walked into the bathroom and flung it into the toilet in disgust. He tossed in the rest of the pack and watched them swirl away with faint regret. In spite of himself, he had to give a snort of laughter. Nothing like a reformed sinner to see the errors of others, he reminded himself dryly. Like those ex-smokers who went around preaching on the evils of cigarettes, he'd fallen into the role of sanctimonious do-gooder, trying to save Paige from herself.

Except that she had the right to make her own way in this world, to make her own mistakes. To deny her that was to deny her everything that was important and real in life. There were going to be times when she was going to hurt. And there was nothing he could do but stand by and hurt with her. And perhaps be there for her when she needed a smile and a hug. When it was all over, he'd still be there. Waiting. And maybe *that*, he decided with a flash of insight that startled him, was what love was all about.

He looked at the clock again. Two forty-five. Then he made up his mind, strode back into the bedroom and reached for his briefs.

Paige's bedroom was dark and silent. He breathed in the scent of her perfume greedily as he padded across the carpet toward the bed, nearly tripping over Bub in the dark. The cat fled with a rumbling growl and Marc swore softly, then realized that Paige was awake, watching him silently.

"Sorry," he muttered.

"I was awake." She sounded wary. Puzzled.

Marc stood by the bed for a moment, then sat on the edge with a weary sigh. "I had my little speech all planned before I came up here. Now I can't remember a word." Paige didn't say anything. Her eyes were very wide and dark, and she was clutching the edge of the sheet as though afraid he was going to rip it from her. "You were right," he finally said. "About everything. I've been riding roughshod over your life since the day I busted through that wall, running things as though you were just part of a building contract. I had no right trying to tell you how to operate GingerBread Preserves, and I had no right phoning the bank about your loan." He met her eyes for the first time. "I knew you wouldn't take money from me, but I wanted to help, Paige."

Still, she didn't say anything. Marc reached out and brushed a tendril of hair from her cheek. Her skin was like satin, and he ached to hold her. "That's not the only reason, of course. It was more selfish than that. I knew you'd never marry me until you were sure that GingerBread would be successful and you felt you'd finally gotten your life under control. It wasn't hard to figure out why—marrying me while things were unsettled in your life and career would be too much like taking the easy way out. Like going home to your parents. But I'm an impatient man. Hell, you know that. I've waited over fifteen years to figure out what I want out of life, and when I finally had all the answers, I didn't want to wait any longer. So I gambled that if you got the money you needed to turn

GingerBread around, you'd figure you'd won. And marry me.'' He smiled wistfully. ''It almost worked.''

''Oh, Marc.'' She closed her eyes, and when she opened them again they were very bright. ''What am I going to do with you?''

''You could always marry me,'' he muttered hopefully.

To his astonishment and relief, she burst out laughing. She sat up and slipped her arms around his neck and Marc hugged her fiercely, scarcely daring to hope he could be this lucky. He buried his face in her hair, drinking in the warmth and scent of her, feeling her breasts against his bare chest even through the filmy stuff of her nightgown.

She rested her cheek on his shoulder. ''Marc, I'm so sorry for all those stupid things I said. I've been lying here in the dark playing them over and over, trying to figure out how to apologize. I acted like such an idiot!''

Marc chuckled comfortably, giving her a squeeze. ''One thing at a time, darling. Stop interrupting my apology with your apology. I haven't finished telling you what an idiot I've been. We'll get to you later.''

Paige gave a little sob of laughter, and when he felt something wet trickle down his chest, he realized she was crying. He held her tightly, thinking of her lying here alone, crying silently in the darkness. ''I said some pretty stupid things, too sweetheart. Angry things. They didn't mean anything.'' He nuzzled her neck and throat, feeling her body heat soak through him. He caressed her back and shoulders, fascinated at the textures under his hands as they moved from the cool satin of her nightgown to the warmth of her skin.

She lifted her head, and in the next moment her mouth was under his, opening to him, drawing him into its sweet warmth. She caught one of his hands in hers and placed it on her breast, arching her back slightly to press it against his palm.

"No, Paige." Marc wrapped his arms around her and held her tightly, ignoring the hammering of his own heart, the vital response of his own body. "I don't want to be just your lover. I want to be your husband. And you're not ready to make that decision yet. I understand that now. You've got too many other things to worry about before we come to that one." He smiled and cupped her face, brushing her hair back with his hands. "I was wrong about the way I went about that loan, Paige. I don't want to be wrong about this. You have to make the decision—I can't do it for you." She opened her lips to say something, but Marc laid his fingers across them. "It would be just as wrong for me to sweet-talk you into believing you're ready to marry me as it would be for me to tell you how to run GingerBread. That ring will be waiting for you. When you're ready to put it back on, you'll know it." He kissed her again, then slipped out of her embrace before all his good intentions went out the window. "Good night, Paige."

After Marc had gone, Paige lay in the darkness, staring up at the ceiling for a long, long while. How, she asked herself calmly, had she ever let that aggravating, lovable man become such an indispensable part of her life? He'd bullied her, read her mail, answered her phone, meddled in every corner and niche of her life. And he'd stolen her heart when she wasn't looking.

The bed dipped as Bub jumped up beside her, purring softly. "Oh, hell," she whispered to the cat. "I suppose you realize I love him, don't you?" But the cat merely purred, as though the possibility didn't worry him in the least. "And I also suppose," she grumbled as she sat up and slid out of bed, "that I'm not going to be able to get any sleep until I tell him so."

Making her way through Marc's darkened living room and up the wide, curving stairs to his second-floor master suite was like negotiating an obstacle course, but Paige finally got through the moving boxes, cartons of building supplies, pieces of lumber and stray tools with nothing more serious than a stubbed toe. Bub trotted beside her, grumbling loudly at this unprecedented nighttime activity.

She heard Marc's delightful baritone chuckle as she made her way cautiously across the huge expanse of gray carpeting to his bed. "It would be a damned sight easier if we just knocked another hole in the wall and turned this into one big bedroom." Marc lifted up onto one elbow and grinned at her, naked but for the sheet draped carelessly across his hips.

Paige tucked one foot under her and sat on the edge of his bed, laughing. "I know. Just don't ask me to marry you again, though. I might agree, and then look at the mess we'd be in. You just got all these walls finished."

"Walls can be knocked down, Paige."

"Yes." She took his hand in hers and stared down at it, tracing each knuckle with her finger. "I've been so busy putting them up to keep people from helping me that I forgot it's sometimes nice to knock them down." She looked at him through her lashes, smiling shyly. "I think the word you used was 'obsessed.'"

"That may have been a little heavy."

"It was also correct. Somehow my perspective got twisted in the last couple of years. I was so caught up with *where* I was headed that I lost sight of *why*." His fingers curled around hers and Paige put her other hand on his, taking a deep breath. "I need help, Marc," she said softly. "It's getting away from me, and I'm scared I'm going to lose everything. Even with...with your money, I don't know if I can hang on to it." To Paige's surprise, saying the words aloud had been quite painless. Actually, it felt very good. She found herself smiling and looked up to meet his eyes. "It's strange, but I always thought asking for help was giving up control. Or admitting failure. But it's just saying that you trust someone, isn't it?"

"You are really something, you know that?" he murmured, lifting her hand to his mouth and kissing her fingertips one at a time. "Are you serious? About wanting my help, I mean?"

"Yes."

She said it without the slightest hesitation or doubt, and Marc looked at her. Then he nodded and sat up, pushed a couple of pillows behind him and leaned back against the headboard. "I don't know anything about the food business, Paige."

"No, but you're a good businessman, and I trust your judgment. You've already hinted at problems you see that I don't. Just tell me everything that you think may give me trouble, and I'll take it from there. After all," she added, gently teasing him, "it's your money."

"Okay," he sighed, "you asked for it. First of all, your product list is way too big, too varied. Instead of trying to make a little bit of everything for everybody, specialize. Choose three, maybe four, of your best products and forget the rest for a while. There'll be lots of time to branch out and expand once you're established and have built up a good customer following. You don't have the time or the money or enough hands to do it all now. Put that time, money and energy into making the best damned ginger marmalade or spaghetti sauce or whatever that you can. And buy only the best quality supplies you can. Forget cheap jars. Buy those pretty etched ones we were looking at earlier this week. And get three-color labels made up, elegant ones. Preferably," he added with a smile, "with glue."

Paige laughed quietly, squeezing his fingers. "Okay, I'm with you so far."

"Set up a schedule you can live with, and stick to it. Right now you're running in circles, making deliveries every day, then racing home to make up the next day's orders. And if I were you, I'd consider changing the name. GingerBread Preserves is homey and comfortable—but you don't want homey and comfortable. Not in Cabbagetown. The market here is sophisticated, upwardly mobile and image-conscious. They want quality and they're willing to pay for it. Pick a name that's simple and elegant and with a touch of class. Like the lady herself. Something like…how about just *Paige's*?"

"*Paige's.*" She said it a couple more times, weighing it, testing it. Then she nodded decisively. "You're right. I like it. I should have seen it myself.…"

"When was the last time you gave yourself five uninterrupted minutes to contemplate anything?" he said. "Which is another thing you'd better think about changing. Take those five uninterrupted minutes now and then. Get to know your son again. He's growing up fast, Paige, and you don't want to miss a minute of it. And take some time out for yourself, too."

"And?"

"That'll get you started. I have a few other ideas, but they're just details, things you can incorporate at any time." He smiled, looking speculatively at her. "But there's one you're not going to like much."

"Such as?"

"Ask your father for some advice. Or borrow some money from him." Paige sucked in a breath to protest and he held up his hand. "Ten dollars. Fifty. The amount doesn't matter. His little girl's growing away from him, Paige, and he's terrified that he's losing her. You're all he's got. Just make him feel as though you still need him now and again, that's all." He grinned suddenly, looking very boyish in the dim light. "And as long as we're on the topic of fragile male egos, I won't complain if you pretend to need me once in a while, too."

Paige smiled, reaching out to trace the curve of his lower lips with her finger. "I don't need to pretend, Marc."

"You'd better get out of here," he whispered, slipping his hand behind her head and pulling her gently toward him. He kissed her slowly and deeply, groaning a little as he finally drew his mouth from hers and released her. "I managed to resist you once tonight, but I wouldn't lay bets that I could do it again."

Paige chuckled throatily. She walked toward the door, then paused there to look back at him. "Did it taste good?"

"Did what taste good?"

"The cigarette," she said guiltily, knowing she was the reason he'd broken his vow not to smoke again. "I tasted it when you kissed me."

Marc grinned wryly. "It tasted like hell. I threw it out after two drags."

"Good." Paige smiled. "I like a man with strong willpower."

That husky chuckle came from out of the darkness. "You're my only vice these days, lady. Now, get out of here before that willpower gives out altogether."

She'd done it.

Paige closed her ledger and leaned back in the chair with a smile. For the first time since GingerBread Preserves had gone from dream to reality, she'd ended a month in the black.

Not GingerBread anymore, she reminded herself with a chuckle. Paige's. But whatever she chose to call it these days, there was no denying that her small company was not only holding its head above water; it was thriving.

She'd halved her product list since her talk with Marc nearly a month ago. It had been hard to decide what to let go, but she'd finally realized that her preserves, jams and chutneys were what she loved making best. Sadly, she'd packed away her spice mill and sauce labels and had told her customers that her spaghetti sauce and barbecue spice weren't available anymore. To her surprise, she hadn't lost any customers. In fact, some of them had been openly relieved that the choice had narrowed, and had doubled their orders for her jams or compotes.

"That's the last of them." The tiny black-haired young woman standing in Paige's kitchen pulled off her rubber gloves and tossed them across the stack of just-washed dishes with a grin. "I'm going to be glad when you can afford a dishwasher!"

"Next month, Heather," Paige promised with a smile. Marc had spent three solid days persuading her that she couldn't afford not to hire someone to help her with the housework. And since Heather had started coming in three times a week, not a day had gone by that Paige hadn't silently thanked him.

"I was going to clean up Tyler's room this afternoon. Or is there something else you'd like me to do first?"

Paige gave a peal of laughter. "If you're going to clean up Tyler's room, you deserve a medal for bravery above and beyond, not more work! If you're not out by noon tomorrow, I'll send in the Marines." She shoved her chair back and stood up, carrying her coffee cup into the kitchen. "Going to the movies with Greg again tonight?"

Heather blushed prettily. "Actually, we're going to a rock concert at Maple Leaf Gardens."

"Sounds pretty serious." Paige drank the last swallow of coffee, watching Heather over the cup rim with amusement. Oh, to be sixteen and in love, she mused. "If you want to leave early to get ready, go ahead."

"Oh, no, that's all right," Heather assured her hastily. "I need every penny I can make this summer if I'm going to go to college next fall."

Paige laughed again, putting her empty cup in the sink. "I wasn't planning on paying you any less for the day, Heather. If you manage to make some headway in Tyler's room this afternoon, you deserve a couple of hours off. Besides," she added with a mischievous smile, "if I were going on a date with a hunk like Greg d'Angelo, I'd want an extra few minutes to get ready."

Heather blushed furiously again, and Paige hid her smile by turning away. "By the way, if you find a tattered old yellow blanket with the binding all worn off while you're up there, don't throw it out."

"You mean Tyler's old baby blanket? I washed it last week and packed it away in that trunk of baby stuff you keep in the attic."

Paige looked around in surprise. "Does he know?"

"Sure. I asked him if he wanted it and he said no, that he was too grown-up for a baby blanket now." Heather smiled. "He's sure growing up fast. I've noticed a difference just in the two weeks I've been working here."

Paige nodded, gazing out the patio doors to where Tyler was industriously pulling nails out of a stack of old boards. He was wearing a carpenter's apron six sizes too large for him, and the claw hammer he was working with would have been adequate for a lumberjack, but he'd been out there for hours now, carefully dropping each salvaged nail into the tin beside him. What Marc actually did with the old nails, she had no idea, but the job kept Tyler happy and busy. Bub lay stretched out beside him, dozing in the late-morning sun.

"I'll make his lunch now," Heather said behind her. "Would you like something to eat, too? You've been working on those books all morning."

Paige shook her head, then turned around, smiling. "Why don't you make up a picnic lunch and take Tyler over to the park? It's such a beautiful day it seems a shame to waste it by staying inside. Tyler's room will last another day."

"Are you sure?" Heather looked undecided.

"I'm sure," Paige told her firmly, untying the apron around Heather's waist and tossing it aside. "Go!"

"But what about you?"

"Me?" Paige paused with her hand on the sliding screen door to the deck, glancing around with a smile. "I'm going up on the roof for a while."

She slid the screen closed behind her, smiling at Heather's astonished expression. Tyler looked up and grinned happily at her and she bent down and gave him a kiss.

"Can I come wif you, Mommy?"

"Not this time, Tyler. I'm going up on the roof."

"Onna roof?" he echoed, his face holding the same astonishment as Heather's. "Marc's onna roof."

"Yes, I know." Paige gazed up the long ladder leaning against the house and took a deep breath, then wiped her hands on her thighs and stepped up onto the first rung.

She was probably crazy, she told herself calmly. She'd probably kill herself before she got even halfway up there. But she'd realized something this morning as she'd updated the figures in her ledger: There was one thing better than succeeding. And that was the discovery that there was strength in being able to accept help when it was lovingly offered. And even more exciting was the possibility that she could succeed in anything she set her mind to. Including love. And she just didn't want to wait any longer to tell the man who'd taught her.

To Paige's relief, Marc was still on the flat part of the roof over the kitchen, replacing shingles on the upsloping part that rose to a peak toward the center of the house. He was stripped to the waist and gleaming with sweat. His broad back had turned a deep ruddy bronze under the blazing sun. Smiling to herself, she slipped her arms around his narrow waist and kissed him between the shoulder blades.

Marc gave a startled oath and jumped, knocking over the small bucket at his elbow. Shingle nails tinkled across the entire roof. "What the—?"

"Oops, sorry." Paige gave a merry laugh and started working her kisses around his ribs to his chest. "Hi."

He gazed down at her, looking mildly stunned. "Where did you come from?"

"Oh, I just thought I'd pop up and tell you I made twelve dollars and eighteen cents profit today."

His sunburned face broke into a broad grin and he wrapped his arms around. "Congratulations. May I take you out to dinner tonight to celebrate?"

"Sure," she said very casually. She ran her hands up his sweat-soaked chest, fingers splayed. "Actually, I came up here to ask you something."

"Ask." He grinned at her, arms tightening.

Paige dug her fingernails into his chest impatiently. The sunlight glinting off the emerald on her left hand nearly blinded her, but Marc seemed totally oblivious to it. "Well. In the last couple of months, you've asked me to marry you about a hundred times, give or take a few."

"Yeah." Marc's eyes narrowed slightly.

"And," Paige went on, turning her hand this way and that admiringly. "I just wondered if you really meant it."

He saw the ring finally. He reached up and clasped her wrist almost roughly, turning her hand so he could look down at it. When his eyes finally lifted to meet hers, they were stunned. "Are you…?"

"…asking you to marry me?" she asked cheekily. "Yes. If you'll have me."

"Have you?" he asked with a bark of laughter, grabbing her and pulling her into his arms. "Lady, I'd have you right here and now if I could be sure Pop or Gabe weren't going to show up any minute."

He dropped his mouth over hers with a satisfying thoroughness.

Paige sighed and slid her arms around his neck. "I love you," she whispered.

"And you came all the way up here to tell me that?"

"It seemed like a good idea at the time."

He kissed her again, even more thoroughly this time. "I've been going through hell this past month, seeing you every day, wanting you."

Paige smiled up at him mischievously. "Heather's taking Tyler to the park for the afternoon."

"Really?" His eyes widened with interest. "All afternoon?"

"All afternoon."

"Are you inviting me down for an afternoon of illicit pleasures, ma'am?" His eyes glowed.

"Of the most lascivious kind. Interested?"

"As I said," he growled, starting to edge her toward the ladder, "try to stop me." He grinned down at her. "You sure about this?"

"Absolutely."

Marc threw his head back and gave a rebel yell that startled two garbage collectors following their big truck down the back lane. They stared up through the tree branches, and Marc cupped his hands around his mouth and bellowed, "She's going to marry me!"

The taller of the two shifted his cigar to the other side of his mouth and touched his cap. "Kiss her for me, buddy!"

"Marc!" Paige gave a squeak of laughing protest

as Marc's arms went around her and he lifted her against him.

"Kiss me, wench. The peasants demand it."

"You are such an idiot!" she told him fondly, tangling her fingers in his hair and tugging his mouth down to hers. "I love you, Marc d'Angelo."

"Does that mean you're going to marry me?"

"Try to stop me."

"Not in a million years," he murmured, bringing his mouth down sweetly over hers. In the back lane, the driver of the garbage truck gave the horn a long, raucous blast, and the two collectors applauded.

"Are you sure that wall isn't load-bearing?" Paige asked her new husband for the tenth time in fifteen minutes. She bit the inside of her cheek nervously as she watched her youngest brother-in-law draw the sledgehammer back for another swing. Greg brought it around smoothly and another section of bricks bulged outward, then spilled across the living room floor.

Marc's arm tightened reassuringly around her shoulders. "Positive. Getting cold feet?"

"About you, no. About the wall, sort of." She looked up at him. "I just have visions of the whole house caving in around our ears one night...." She stopped, blushing, as Marc's face broke into a teasing smile.

"If this old house were going to cave in because of our rowdy lovemaking, sweetheart, we'd have brought it down long before now."

"That's not what I meant at all," she protested with a laugh, giving his waist a hug.

"No more walls between us, sweetheart," Marc said softly, turning to take her in his arms. "Chestnut Manor's waited twenty years to be made whole again."

"Me, too," she whispered against his mouth.

And as the last bricks of the common wall between both halves of Chestnut Manor fell, Paige knew that the last wall between her and happiness had come tumbling down.

*   *   *   *   *

SPECIAL EDITION™

Emotional, compelling stories that capture the intensity of living, loving and creating a family in today's world.

Modern, passionate reads that are powerful and provocative.

nocturne

Dramatic and sensual tales of paranormal romance.

Romances that are sparked by danger and fueled by passion.

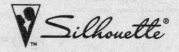

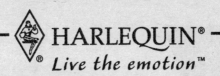

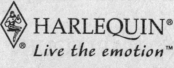

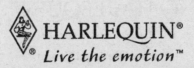